The Long Siesta

The Long Siesta

NICK SWEET

Grey Cells Press

www.greycellspress.co.uk

Paperback ISBN 978-1-909374-74-4
Epub 978-1-909374-75-1
Kindle 978-1-909374-96-6

Cover art by B.Lloyd

Typesetting by handebooks.co.uk

Grey Cells Press
An Imprint of Holland House Books

Holland House
47 Greenham Road
Newbury
Berkshire
RG14 7HY
United Kingdom

www.greycellspress.co.uk

Dedicated to my father, Ronald Joseph Sweet,
in loving memory.

1

TERCIO DE VARAS

The matador *offered the cape and the bull stood stock still. Then it charged, and it looked for a moment as though the bull would gore the* matador. *But when it hooked upwards with its horns, it found only the cape and empty air.*

CHAPTER 1

July 1998, Seville

The victim had been forced over the back of an armchair and tied. There was a lot of dried blood, as well as some excrement, on the backs of his legs. The legs themselves were white and spindly, practically hairless. Thick green varicose veins snaked their way down the backs of the calves and thighs. They were the legs of a very old man. The handle of a kitchen knife protruded from between the flat, white buttocks.

Inspector Jefe Velázquez got down on his haunches to look at the victim's face, the man's cheek resting against the worn leather upholstery of the chair. The gag would have prevented his screams from being heard, but the eyes told of unspeakable terror and agony. Velázquez didn't recognize him.

He began to inspect the head, bald save for a tonsure of grey hair and patched with age spots and moles. The wispy hair at the back of the head had some blood in it. Now dry, it had trickled down the victim's neck and stained his dog collar.

Who'd want to kill a priest? Velázquez wondered. And why? Could this be politically motivated? Certainly there were people out there who blamed the clergy for just about every disaster that had ever been visited on the country, right from the days of Torquemada down to the latest child abuse scandal.

The stench of the victim's excrement had begun to attract the attention of a number of flies. He laid the back of his hand against the victim's cheek. Still warm. Can't have been killed very long ago, he concluded. Question of an hour or two at most. Maybe less. Although he'd need the *Médico Forense* to confirm that.

Velázquez took a pair of nitrile gloves from his breast pocket, put them on and gently parted the bloodied hair. The scalp was badly bruised, indicating that the murderer came at him from behind with a hard solid object. Must've hit him first, then used the knife afterwards.

Always a chance the killer had left whatever he hit the victim with at the crime scene. Velázquez searched the room, just in case, but failed to find what he was looking for. Next he went through the victim's pockets, found a wallet and inspected its contents. Some paper money—twenty-five thousand *pesetas* in total—and a number of plastic cards. He took the cards out and looked at them. Three credit cards, a library card, the deceased's *carné de identidad*, and another card bearing the name of the church where the deceased had served.

He had just finished making a note of the deceased's name, the number on his *carné* and the name of the church, when he heard the familiar voice of his number two, Subinspector José Gajardo, talking to the uniform standing guard out in the hallway. Velázquez went and popped his head round the door.

'Got here soon as I could, Boss,' said Gajardo, eyes flashing with excitement. Two years younger than Velázquez at thirty-five, somehow the Inspector Jefe always felt as though the age difference were greater. Question of professional seniority, he supposed.

Looking at his number two, he said, 'Another new suit, is it, José?'

'Sale on over at the Corte Ingles, thought I'd treat myself.' Gajardo smiled and held his arms out to show off his new acquisition. 'What do you reckon?'

The pale grey number fitted the Subinspector's lean athletic frame to a tee. 'Nice,' Velázquez had to admit, feeling underdressed in his black denims and leather jacket. He dismissed the notion from his mind. Fucking crime scene, not a fashion show.

'Been a big accident,' Gajardo said. 'Came the long way round, avoid getting stuck in traffic. Anyway, don't s'pose I've missed much?'

'Vic certainly isn't going anywhere fast, if that's what you mean.'

'So where's the body?'

'In here.' Velázquez pointed, and stood aside to allow Gajardo to pass through the doorway. He wondered once more about the significance of the victim's being a priest. Men of the cloth were supposed to be caring, paternal figures, weren't they? Wasn't that why everyone called them 'Father'? Maybe, but the clergy had done a lot of things down through the years, and there were people who remembered.

When Gajardo saw the victim, his thick black brows rose and squirmed like caterpillars with money trouble, and the word '*Joder*' escaped from the Subinspector's lips in a quiet, involuntary lament that filled the room for an instant like a short prayer. Then he noticed the dog-collar. 'We got an ID, Boss?' The Inspector Jefe nodded and said, 'Name's Father Pedro Moro. Served at Jesús del Gran Poder.' It was over on the Plaza de San Lorenzo, just a stone's throw from the Inspector Jefe's flat, as it turned out, in the Old Quarter.

'I know it.' Difficult to find a grown Sevillano who didn't. 'Want me to call the *Científicos*?'

'Already on their way… so's the Judge.'

Velázquez glanced round the room, which had served as a study. There was a desk over in the far corner, a worn leather sofa matched the easy chair the victim had been strapped to, and shelves crammed with books ran along one wall. Ecclesiastical volumes, bound in Moroccan leather. The rest of the wall space was covered with religious paintings and icons. He recognized one of the oils, a Zurbarán copy: slight figure standing before a number of monks and a woman who looked like a nun. Kinda creepy.

He parted the slats of the venetian blind and peered down from the first-floor window on Calle Viriato, a narrow street bang in the heart of Seville. Two men were going past on the pavement, both dressed in smart business suits. They walked fast, one waving his hands as he talked. Velázquez wondered what those men would think if they saw the murder scene. He had no doubt that they would be shocked, horrified. Things like that just didn't happen here. Not in Seville. Or if they happened at all, then it would be out in the notorious Tres Mil Viviendas, where a good proportion of the city's gypsy population lived. But not in elegant apartment blocks on Calle Viriato, in the heart of well-to-do Campana.

Velázquez took a look round the rest of the flat. The bedroom at the back overlooked a shaded inner courtyard dominated by a fountain, offering respite from the heat. Could almost be the sixteen hundreds, Velázquez thought. Seville for you.

An inspection of the kitchen and small bathroom gave no indication of a violent struggle, or anything that might suggest an intruder's presence. Neither did the lock on the front door show any signs of forced entry.

No sign of the bloodied solid object the killer hit the vic on the back of the head with anywhere, either.

He picked up the telephone, got up the last number that had been called and made a note of it. Then he took out his mobile and called the number, stood looking at the blood on the Turkish rug as he listened to the ringtone. Somebody picked up, and Velázquez said, '*Hola*, I'm Father Pedro.' A woman's voice that was to sex what Verdi was to opera told him he was through to the Express Escort Agency. 'I called a while ago,' he said. 'I'm on Calle Viriato.'

'Yes, we sent a lad round to you over an hour ago. Hasn't he arrived yet?'

'No... what's the name of the lad again?'

'My colleague's just finished her shift, but she should've left a note. Let me have a look.' The line went quiet for a moment; then the woman said, 'Ramón... but it says here you asked for him specifically.'

'Yes, that's right—his name escaped me for a moment.'

'He's not normally late.'

'Where's your office?'

'On Menendez Pelayo... but he's not here, so there's no point in your coming—'

'Give me the number anyway, just in case he doesn't show... I might call over and take a look through your catalogue, if you have one.'

The woman told him and Velázquez wrote it down. 'Probably got caught in traffic,' she said. 'Why don't you give it twenty minutes or so, then call again if he hasn't arrived?'

'Okay.'

The woman hung up, and Velázquez stood there for a moment looking into the helix of the phone like he expected a genie to pop out of it. Then he replaced the receiver, his mind working fast.

'Boss...?'

Velázquez ran a hand through his wavy black hair, already flecked with grey at the sides. 'Seems the priest called an escort agency, made a specific request for a lad called Ramón and they sent him over here.'

'Looks a bit old to be getting up to that sort of thing.'

'Born nineteen twenty... be seventy-eight in December.'

'How'd you know that?'

'Says so on his *carné de identidad*... It was in his pocket.'

'Just goes to show, doesn't it?' Gajardo frowned. 'So this Ramón could be here any moment, then?'

'Could be... unless he's already come and gone.'

'You mean it could've been this Ramón character that—'

'Let's not jump to any rash conclusions, okay?'

Moments later the *Médico Forense,* Juan Gómez, an old friend of Velázquez, came through the door. The two men acknowledged each other, and the Gomez saw the body. *'Joder!* What a mess.'

He slipped on a pair of nitrile gloves, parted the victim's blood-stained buttocks and gently eased out the butcher's knife. A jet of blood spurted out, sullying the *Médico Forense's* chinos. 'Looks like he was shot up the anus first.' He opened his briefcase, produced a thermometer and slipped it under the victim's tongue.

Velázquez said, 'Body's still warm, I noticed.'

Gomez held the thermometer up to the light. 'You're right, Luis... time of death couldn't've been very much more than an hour ago, if that.'

Velázquez glanced at his watch: it was now 20:06. And he'd arrived on the scene himself some twenty minutes ago. But who was it that called to report the murder? He'd been working on a report at his desk in the *Jefatura* when the call came through from his boss, Comisario Alonso, and he'd rushed straight over here. Didn't find anyone waiting at the door on arrival, apart from the two uniformed officers sent ahead. Could've been the killer himself that called it in.

But why would a person kill someone and then call the police to tell them what they'd done?

Just then, the stocky form of the Instructing Judge, Cristobal Montero, entered the room, bringing with him a whiff of Havana cigars and the aura of assurance you would expect from somebody in his position. Judge Cristobal Montero's lips pursed, as if about to bestow a kiss, when he saw the victim. '*Joder!*' He turned to Velázquez. 'What have you got, Inspector Jefe?'

'Vic was hit from behind, tied up and shot up the anus, Judge... then the killer followed up with a kitchen knife.'

'Worried the bullet hadn't done the job... or else to ram the point home, as it were.'

Velázquez looked at the *Médico Forense* and said, 'I'll need you to get the bullet out a.s.a.p., Juan, for Ballistics.'

Gomez nodded. 'Don't worry, Luis, I'll make this one my first priority.'

'Got any leads, Inspector?' Judge Montero wanted to know.

Velázquez quickly brought him up to speed about the escort. 'Think I'll call round there now, see what more I can find out.'

'Shall I come?' asked Subinspector Gajardo.

'No, you stay here, José, in case this Ramón character shows.'

'What shall I do if he does?'

'Want my advice,' Velázquez said, 'don't turn your back on the guy.'

Velázquez climbed into the Seat Ibiza he'd been driving ever since his old Alfa Romeo was stolen and set off through the narrow streets, the pavements and cafes packed with people, skirted the ancient city walls, passed the Palacio de Justicia, and pulled up outside a rank of shops on Calle Menendez Pelayo. Entered through a doorway that was squeezed in between a boutique and a green grocer's, ran up the stairs to the first floor, and rang the buzzer by the side of a door that had THE EXPRESS ESCORT AGENCY written on it in bold print. '*Diga?*'

'I'm looking for a little company,' Velázquez said, and the girl buzzed him in.

The reception area was shiny-new, with varnished wooden boards and white-painted walls adorned with prints. Velázquez's eye came to rest on one of them. Done in black against a bare white surface, it was a painting of a bull charging at a *matador's* cape. The girl was sitting behind the reception desk, all cello curves and scarlet lipstick. 'Good afternoon, *señor*. Can I help you?' She flashed Velázquez a smile that threatened for a moment to wrap him up in silk and race him through a *pasadoble* in a Ferrari.

Velázquez took out his ID and held it out to the girl, saw her sexy manner wilt like a lily in a hurricane. 'I believe you had a call from a priest a little earlier?'

'That would be Father Pedro... he asked us to send a lad of ours over to keep him company—'

'Lad's name was Ramón, wasn't it?'

'That's right—but what's it to you?'

'I already showed you my ID.'

'Not an answer to my question.'

'The badge means I get to ask the questions,' Velázquez said. 'All you have to do is answer them.'

'I prefer to go in for reciprocal relationships.'

'Seems to me you're working in the wrong place.'

'That supposed to be funny?'

'Give me this Ramón's full name and details.'

The girl shrugged and her chest shrugged along with her under her right violet-coloured top. She looked at her computer screen, tapped a few keys, scribbled on a pad, tore the sheet off and handed it to Velázquez, then leaned with her elbows on the wooden desk so that the Inspector Jefe got an eyeful. He looked at the address, then said, 'This *chico* Ramón offers sex in return for cash, I take it?'

The girl merely smiled at Velázquez.

And kept smiling.

And her chest kept smiling along with her.

'What address was this Ramón asked to go to?'

The girl looked back at the screen, scribbled on the pad again and handed it to Velázquez. Father Pedro's address on Calle Viriato, as he had expected.

'This Father Pedro a regular client?'

The girl shook her head. 'His first time with us.'

'Got a photo of Ramón?'

'Can print one off for you, if you like.'

'Thanks.'

The Inspector Jefe looked at the mug shot, then folded it and put the piece of paper in his breast pocket.

'Anything else I can do for you, Inspector Jefe?'

'I'll let you know if there is.' He made for the door.

'Aren't you going to stick around?'

Velázquez said 'Let's save it for a rainy day, shall we?' Then heard the girl say, 'Torrential rain's forecast for tomorrow, so don't leave the house without your mackintosh.'

CHAPTER 2

Inspector Jefe Velázquez tried the address the girl had given him for Ramón Ochoa, but nobody was home; so he went back to his car, took out his mobile and called Subinspector Gajardo. When Gajardo picked up, Velázquez said, 'Our friend Ramón show yet?'

''Fraid not, Boss… what do you want me to do now?'

'Hook up with Serrano, Pérez and Merino, and see what they've turned up, if anything.'

'What've they been doing, Boss?'

'Knocking on doors,' Velázquez said. 'You know the routine—make sure they've talked to all of the people who live in the building. If anyone was out when they called earlier, then go back and try again. Once everyone in the building's been spoken to, get them to start calling on people in the neighbouring buildings… You can help them out. Call into the local shops, the butcher's and the green grocer's, any bars and cafes in the area. I want to know if anyone saw Father Pedro in the hours leading up to the time he was murdered. And try to find out what kind of man he was, what sort of company he kept, anything you can about his lifestyle… Oh, and give Oficial Merino the mug shot of Ramón Ochoa, and tell him to go round the gay bars… I want to know straightaway if anyone turns anything up, okay.'

They hung up and, some forty minutes later, Velázquez hooked up with Gajardo and the rest of his team, in the building on Calle Viriato. It turned out that nobody the officers had spoken to heard anything. Nobody had heard any screams or noises that might have suggested a violent struggle was taking place in Father Pedro's flat earlier that day.

Nobody had seen anyone enter or leave Father Pedro's place,

either.

Nobody knew whether or not Father Pedro had been gay.

Some people had expressed a degree of surprise at the question, though. What did the man's sexuality have to do with anything? they wanted to know. Besides, what did people see when they looked at a priest? What they wanted to, in most cases, Velázquez figured. Where some people saw a servant of God, others saw a hated enemy. Even in some cases a servant of the guy downstairs.

Velázquez told his team to keep at it, and began knocking on doors himself. Continued to do so until well into the early hours of the morning, then figured he'd go and try Ramón's address once more. Again nobody came to the door when he rang the bell. Instead a little old lady in a dressing gown appeared in the doorway of the neighbouring flat. 'Pilar's not at home,' she said.

'She make a habit of staying out this late?'

The woman's head tilted to one side. 'Don't sound as though you know her all that well.'

'Not married or living with someone, I take it?'

The woman glanced about her, to make sure nobody was eavesdropping. 'She was married, yes, only her husband he cheated on her so she kicked him out.'

'She the one who told you he was unfaithful to her?'

'No, but I heard people say how he gave her a pair of horns, you know.' Her eyes narrowed in a suspicious squint. 'Bit late to be calling on somebody you don't really know, isn't it?'

'Her son, Ramón, I really need to talk to.'

The woman nodded, adjusted her dressing gown. 'Who are you then might I ask?'

Velázquez took out his ID and held it out for the woman to see. She frowned. 'Is Ramón in some sort of trouble?'

'I have reason to believe his life could be in serious danger, *señora*,' Velázquez said. 'So it's in his interest to talk to me.'

'What's the *chico* got himself involved in this time, then?' The woman's eyes were open wide now, like she was greedy for gossip. Velázquez knew the type. Her old man's gone on to bed or else he's gone to a better place; either way the woman's lonely and bored. So she stays up half the night watching the gossip shows, then goes to the café next day and talks about it all with her friends, or failing that with anybody who'll listen to her.

'Afraid I can't say, *señora*.' Velázquez smiled at the woman, sensing that she wanted to talk.

'Pilar's a nurse over at the Macarena hospital, works nights,' she said, sweeping a blotched hand over her perfectly grey hair. 'Won't be back until the morning, then she normally sleeps in until early in the afternoon.'

'What about Ramón?'

'Pilar was only telling me a little earlier, before she left for work, how she hasn't seen him in days… Told me she's so sick and tired of him coming and going as it pleases him, she's changed the lock to stop him getting in.'

'Sounds a bit drastic.'

'I would too, if I was in her shoes… Tried talking to him,' she said, but it's a waste of time. You know what they can be like at that age.'

'Sounds like there isn't much communication between them.'

'Just throwing water into the sea, trying to talk to Ramón, Pilar said.' The woman gave Velázquez a knowing look. 'Doesn't mind him coming to stay as long as he likes, she said, but she's fed up with the way he uses the place like it's a hotel. Shows up at four in the morning and starts making lots of noise, fixing himself a plate of pasta or whatever it is. Pilar gets back from work, or else wakes up on her day off, and the sink's full of dishes, he's left his plate on the table in the living room and there's food stuck to it, the TV's been on since he came in with the volume turned up full blast so none of the neighbours've been able to get any sleep, and to cap it all Ramón's puked all over the carpet. You get the picture.'

'He always like that?'

'Pretty much... except when he's in one of his really troublesome moods.'

'What's he do then?'

'Comes round asking her for money,' she said. 'Well, demanding it more like.'

'Pilar tell you all this?'

'Doesn't have to, you can hear it all through the walls... Ramón shouting like a *toro* about what he's going to do if she doesn't cough up.'

'You mean he threatens to hit her?'

'Threatens to tie some heavy stones to his ankles 'n throw himself in the river more like.'

'He a junky?'

'So they say,' she said. 'Not that Pilar's ever used the word talking with me, you know.'

'She always give him money when he asks for it?'

'She's a mother at the end of the day,' the woman said. 'She loves that boy more than anything in the world.' She glanced about her quickly, like a spy in some old B movie. 'I know for a fact that he's shown up here before now and stolen stuff from the flat when Pilar's been out.'

'What kind of stuff?'

'Anything he can get his hands on... even walked off with the television set one time.'

'Saw him leave with it, did you?'

'No, but I know somebody who did.' She smiled. 'Block like this, the walls have eyes and ears, you know what I mean... Can't blow your nose without there's somebody seen or heard you.'

'How they get,' Velázquez said. 'Do anything to get their fix.'

'"Ramón wants to sleep here," Pilar says to me, "then he's gonna have to tell me he's coming beforehand from now on, and he's got to start pullin' his weight more and smarten up his act."'

'Can't say I blame her by the sound of things.'

'Pilar's a good woman, and she's been a good mother to that

chico, too... but there's a limit to everything.'

'Sure is.' Velázquez glanced at his Swatch: it had just gone two a.m., perhaps time to call it a night. He thanked the woman for her help, left the building, went back to his car and set off, the narrow streets mostly empty now save for a few late-night revellers.

There were no parking spaces left when he got home, so he had to drive round searching for one; ended up all the way down on Jesús del Gran Poder, by the colony of pimps, prostitutes and pushers, the Alameda de Hercules only a short walk away. Even then he had to leave the car with two wheels up on the pavement. He worried that the car might share the same destiny as his beloved Alfa Romeo, and get stolen; but he was dog-tired and couldn't be arsed to search for another parking space.

Velázquez was feeling like shit and needed a fix badly as he entered the block on Calle Teodosio. He ran upstairs, let himself into the flat and shut the front door quietly, then padded through the living room and along the hallway to the bedroom. Opened the door slowly, careful not to make a noise, and saw that Pe was lying on her back and lost to the land of Nod. The light was still on and a book had fallen onto the floor by her side: she must have fallen asleep in the middle of her reading again. Velázquez, prone more to bouts of insomnia, envied Pe this ability of hers to drop off anytime, anywhere. But *boy*, she was beautiful, with her long black hair all sprayed out on the pillow like that; and she was blowing little bubbly air-kisses through her pink lips as she breathed.

Returning to the living room, he took the baggie and the syringe from their hiding place, behind his selection of true-crime and history books on the shelf in the corner, went into the kitchen, put some of the heroin in a spoon and heated it up. Then he filled the syringe, rolled up his shirt sleeve and pumped his arm. He experienced a moment of intense pleasure when the needle went in.

After quickly washing the needle, he slipped it into his jacket pocket, along with what was left in the baggie. *Joder*, he thought, this is crazy. *I'm* fucking crazy. Except he wasn't.

He was an addict. Had been since he'd been abducted by Bill and the Black Lady. Quite who the pair were Velázquez had yet to find out. But he was determined to do so, if it was the last thing he ever did.

They'd marked him, changed him in ways that he hadn't wanted to be changed. It would come back to him at night, and he'd wake up in a cold sweat, remembering. They'd had him tied to the chair, blindfolded. The Black Lady giving him all this spiel about coming over from New Orleans. Bullshit, all of it. Velázquez doubted she was even 'black'. Like it was all a big laugh for them and he was the butt of the joke. Then the guy who called himself Bill would put the needle in, and everything would start to be fun. For a while, anyway...

Isn't my fault I've got a habit, he told himself. I didn't choose to get myself hooked.

He wondered how long he was going to keep on like this. Knew he couldn't keep using the same old excuse forever.

Time I did something about it, he thought.

Difficult thing was trying to keep his addiction a secret from everyone.

I've got to get off it, he told himself. He'd go to the doctor and get some methadone, start injecting that instead. The only way.

Hardly go cold turkey, he thought, and run a team of homicide cops at the same time. Some bulls were just too big and dangerous to take by the horns.

Funny how ordinary and *normal* it had begun to feel.

He ran the cold water tap and washed his face at the sink, then checked on Pe again, just to make sure she was still asleep.

What she didn't know couldn't hurt her, he thought.

He found the bottle of single malt in the drinks cabinet, poured himself a large one. Kicked his loafers off, threw his jacket over the back of a chair and sat on the leather sofa with his feet up on the glass coffee table, running through the case in his mind, trying to work out what might have happened. Wondering if there was some line of enquiry he'd overlooked.

It was coming up to three-thirty a.m. by the time Velázquez finally turned in, and he slept fitfully. One of those nights when he kept tossing and turning, and the crime scene featured in his dreams, only somehow everything was transformed.

The alarm went off at seven thirty the following morning. He got up, washed and dressed, drank a strong coffee and left the flat. Found the Seat Ibiza parked where he'd left it, started her up and set off. At this hour, there was a pleasant cool breeze blowing, and the streets were still relatively free of pedestrians and traffic. Of course all of that would change within an hour or so, and by midday the pavements would be hot as a frying pan.

Seville is always beautiful—but at this hour, before the traffic of the day began, it was a poem awash with golden tranquillity and ancient mysticism: the sun casting its net in the Guadalquivir, its reflection shimmering over the surface like the scales of a thousand mermaids; the medieval *Torre de Oro*, casting its own golden reflection on the river; on the other side stood the whitewashed Baroque *plaza de toros*, La Maestranza, the oldest bullring in the world, while away in the distance, dominating the skyline with its graceful presence, was the greatest architectural achievement of the Almohads, the minaret of the Giralda. But Velázquez was in no mood to notice such things. Seville might be a symphony for the senses for some, but it was wasted on him. He agreed with Byron, though: you couldn't find better oranges or women anywhere. Velázquez loved the sharp, fresh smell of the fruit that could envelope the city like a poetic aroma at times, conjuring up thoughts of love. As for women: Pe Naranjo was the Best, to his mind. Had been for these past four years or more. Besides, she'd kill him if she ever caught him straying.

Agente Serrano and Oficial Merino were both busy working at their desks when Velázquez entered the office. 'Nice and early,' the Inspector Jefe observed. 'That's what we like.'

As he booted up his computer, a *'Buenos dias'* came from the doorway and Subinspector Gajardo came striding into the office. Neither Serrano nor Merino looked up. But they both did moments later, when Agente Sara Pérez—blonde, twenty-five and stunning—came hurrying in. Her pinstriped trouser suit, doubtless intended to smooth out her natural curves and neutralize her innate feminine charms, failed most thrillingly to achieve its desired effect. Admiration and lust swept across the faces of Serrano and Merino, while Gajardo made a show of not noticing her. As for Velázquez, he didn't bother to put on any act: he really didn't notice Agente Pérez come in.

'Okay,' he growled from his desk, 'now everyone's here you'd better all drop everything and get out and pick up where you left off last night.'

Agente Serrano blew out his cheeks.

'Don't look so excited, Jorge.'

'Sorry, Boss, it's just that—'

'You don't like going out knocking on doors, prefer to be doing something else, I know. So would everyone else. Knocking on doors isn't exciting. It's what salesmen do, and you don't see Mel Gibson do a whole lot of it in *Lethal Weapon*. ... But just because Hollywood can't find any space for it doesn't mean to say it hasn't got to be done. Do I make myself clear?'

'Boss.' Serrano hung his head apologetically.

'Come on, then, the four of you,' Velázquez barked. 'Let's show Clint Eastwood and Mel Gibson how to do it.' He paused a moment, and grinned at his team. 'Get out there and make my day.'

The Inspector Jefe drove at a slow crawl through traffic thick as treacle over to Forensics, where he tracked down Raúl Almonte, head of the *Científico* team. Velázquez didn't have any time for the man, on account of his attitude. Short skinny guy with a big ego, acted like it was all down to him and his team whether any murder cases got solved. Velázquez said hello, asked him if he could see the knife.

'Sure.' Almonte opened a drawer and brought it out. It was in a transparent bag that had been labelled.

'Any prints on the handle?'

Almonte shook his head, ran a hand through his short brown hair. 'No DNA, either, I'm afraid.' He stood with his arms crossed, looking bored.

Velázquez held up the knife in the plastic bag and took a good look at it. 'Standard bread knife,' he said, and wondered if the killer had brought it onto the crime scene with him or found it in the kitchen.

'Mind if I take this with me?'

Almonte shrugged. 'Finished with it here.'

'Thanks.'

Velázquez went down to the dissecting lab, found Gómez stooped over the body of the murder victim.

'Morning, Juan. Looks like you're busy.'

'Know what they say, Luis,' Gómez said. 'No rest for the wicked and all that.'

'Starting to sound like a priest.'

Gómez looked up at Velázquez over the steel frame of his glasses, perched on his rather sizeable nose. 'God forbid.'

Velázquez glanced at the body of the victim on the dissecting table, already cut open from throat to pelvis. 'Don't be shy— take a good look,' Gómez grinned. 'What we're all made of. Any one of these vital organs packs up, we pack up with it.'

'Happy thought.'

Gómez went back to digging around inside the body. 'Bullet's been sent down to Ballistics, case you're wondering,' he said without looking up.

'Any evidence of intercourse having taken place?'

Gómez shook his head. 'There's an indentation on the back of the skull, consistent with a blow struck with a solid blunt instrument—but you already know that.'

'I've got to go.'

'Must have a drink sometime.'

'Yeah, I'll call you.'

Velázquez left the building and drove back to the crime scene, parked with two wheels up on the narrow pavement on Calle Viriato, already packed with parked cars and pedestrians. The sun was shining out of a clear blue sky. It wasn't really hot yet, but it soon would be.

He let himself in with the spare key he'd had made, slipping on a pair of nitrile gloves as he ran up the stairs and entered the flat. Made straight for the kitchen, opened the cutlery drawer and emptied it out onto the Formica worktop. He took all the knives he could find and put them into a carrier bag, then left. Headed down to the end of Viriato, turned up Amor de Dios, traversed the Plaza del Duque, with the tourists sitting on the benches there feeding the pigeons, and entered the Corte Ingles, best place to buy just about anything as long as you didn't mind paying full whack for it.

Made straight for the cutlery department, and had the manager there take a look at the murder exhibit and the set of cutlery. 'I need to know if this knife here would've been part of a set with the other cutlery,' Velázquez said.

The man examined the knife, still in its sheath of plastic, then turned his attention to some of the other knives Velázquez had brought with him. 'Yes,' he said finally, 'this knife in the plastic bag is part of a set, along with several of the others you have shown me.'

'Do you sell a set like this here?'

'Yes we do, as a matter of fact.' The man came out from behind the counter and led Velázquez along one of the aisles, then stopped and pointed to a set that was on display. 'Here.'

'You mean to say this is the very same set?'

'It is indeed.' The man reached out and took a long bread knife from the box. 'And this is the same model of knife as the one you showed me.'

Velázquez drove over to Ramón Ochoa's address once again. A woman in her fifties, dressed in jeans and a pink T-shirt, came to the door. She said, '*Hola,*' and looked at Velázquez out of tired brown eyes underscored by dark bags.

'Are you Señora Pilar Ochoa—Ramón's mother?'

'That's right... but why are you asking?'

'I called round twice yesterday, but nobody answered.'

'My long shift.' She gave him a slant-eyed look. 'But who are you, anyway?'

Velázquez took out his ID and held it up. Señora Ochoa squinted at it. 'What d'you want with my Ramón?'

'Just want to talk to him, that's all.'

'Well, he's not here.'

'Any idea when he'll be back?'

Pilar Ochoa shrugged. 'Haven't seen him for a few days.'

'Where's he gone?'

'No idea...'

'That usual for him—to disappear for a few days at a time?'

'He's a grown man of twenty-five, comes and goes as he pleases.'

'He got a partner, or anyone he hangs out with?'

'Nobody he's told me about.'

Velázquez figured a little improvisation was needed. 'Look, Señora Ochoa, I have reason to believe your son's life may be in danger.'

Her eyes flashed like she'd just woken up. 'What makes you say that?'

'A friend of his has been murdered.'

Her mouth opened, and her hand moved to cover it in an automatic gesture. 'What's the name of this friend?'

'Priest by the name of Father Pedro Mora—and whoever it was may well be after Ramón, too.'

'Why'd they be after Ramón?'

'We have reason to believe the priest was gay,' Velázquez lied. 'And, as I say, that he was friendly with your son.'

Pilar Ochoa frowned, chewing on her lower lip. 'So you think the killer might've been someone who hates gays, is that it?'

'That's one line of enquiry we're considering.'

The woman looked into Velázquez's eyes, as if she were trying to decide whether or not to trust him. Then she said, 'There's a bar that Ramón goes to a lot... *Jorge's*, I think it's called, over on Calle Betis.'

Velázquez thanked the woman for her help. 'And if he comes back then please ask him to give me a call on this number,' he said, and handed her his card.

Velázquez called his number two, but Gajardo wasn't picking up for some reason, so he called Agente Serrano. 'Got anything yet, Jorge?'

'Vic played golf on the morning, Boss, at a club down by Jerez.'

'Who did he play with?'

'German guy by the name of Moeller.'

'Spoken to him yet?'

'On my way to the man's flat now.'

'Find out everything you can about this Moeller character.'

'Okay.'

'Gajardo with you?'

'Gone to the golf club, see if he can turn up anything of interest down there.'

'What about Pérez and Merino?'

'Still knocking on doors.'

'Okay, Jorge, catch you later... and let me know straightaway if you turn anything up.'

'Will do.'

'Oh—and be at the *Jefatura* by three this afternoon, okay. Tell the others, too—I need you all there for a briefing.'

Chapter 3

Velázquez climbed into the Seat Ibiza and set off through the heavy traffic for the *Jefatura* on Blas Infante. Normally he didn't mind driving around Seville, but lately it had become something of a pain. He was missing his old car, the one that had been stolen, the Alfa Romeo. *His* Alfa Romeo. Somehow he was nostalgic for it today, and the fact that he knew his feelings were ridiculous and pointless did nothing to diminish them. He was feeling stressed, too, because he'd arranged to give his team a briefing at three o'clock, and he was going to struggle to get there on time.

Officers Gajardo, Pérez, Merino and Serrano were already there, working at their desks, when he arrived. Velázquez shrugged his black leather jacket off, draped it over the back of his chair, then went and stood in front of the large whiteboard with the mug shot of the vic in the middle of it. 'Okay, everyone,' he said, 'you don't need me to tell you that we're up against a real sicko on this one, and there's nothing to say he won't strike again soon. Now let's stick to the facts and look at what we know.' He turned to face the whiteboard. At the side of the mug shot of the victim, he drew a line at ten o'clock. 'Our vic goes down to El Soleo Golf Club outside Jerez and is seen there playing golf.' He looked at Gajardo. 'Correct, Subinspector?'

'That's right, Boss.'

'You care to fill us in on anything else you learned while you were down there?'

'Vic played a round with a German by the name of Gerhardt Moeller. Both men are well into their seventies, which may explain why they chose to play against each other.'

'Anything else you can tell us?'

'Started around ten in the morning and finished their round

shortly before noon.'

'Okay.' Velázquez drew another line at twelve o'clock. Then he added a vertical line to connect the two lines he had previously drawn, and wrote PLAYED GOLF WITH GERHARDT MOELLER along it. 'Were they joined by a third party?'

'No third party, Boss.'

Velázquez turned back to Serrano. 'You spoke to Moeller, Jorge. What sort of impression did he make on you?'

'Seemed like a pretty normal kind of old guy.'

'*Normal*, huh…?'

'Yeah… ' Serrano shrugged his heavy shoulders.

'Doesn't tell us a lot, Agente. I think we can do better than that.'

Serrano frowned. 'Guy's German but speaks very good Spanish, only with an accent.'

'Seems educated, then?'

'I should say so, yes, most certainly,' Serrano nodded. 'Got a nice enough flat off Calle Feria. Just the one bedroom, but the place was neat and tidy, you know.'

'So killers don't know how to clean up, is that it?'

'Not what I meant.'

'Good, because you should know as well as anyone that we need to beware of making sweeping generalizations.'

Merino laughed, keen to be in the Inspector Jefe's good books.

'What job did the man do before he retired?'

'Said he used to work in a bank and that he knew Father Pedro through the church.'

'What time did he last see Father Pedro?'

'Says he parted company with him shortly after two p.m. Says they had lunch together at the Sardinero, bar on the *plaza* outside the Iglesia del Gran Poder… Said goodbye there, after Moeller picked up the tab and Father Pedro disappeared into the church.'

'Manage to get anyone to corroborate that?'

'Waiter remembered serving them,' Serrano replied. 'He couldn't be totally exact about the time, but knew it was before quarter past two they both left because that was when he left work. Says he had an appointment at the dentist's at two-thirty... He remembered seeing the two men go their separate ways, like Moeller said—Father Pedro going into the church and Moeller going off in the other direction, across the square.'

'And where did Moeller go then?'

'Says he walked back to his flat and stayed there until late in the evening.'

'How late?'

'Just gone ten.'

'By which time the vic was long dead,' Javier Merino said.

'Manage to corroborate any of this?'

Serrano shook his head. 'Only his movements up until he left the Sardinero, Boss.'

'Which could make Moeller a suspect, are we thinking, or what?' Sara Pérez wondered aloud.

'Sure he's a suspect,' Velázquez said, '—along with just about everyone else in this damn city... What about Father Pedro? Any accounting for his movements after that?'

'He talked to a Father Antonio for a while in the church,' Jorge Serrano said. 'Father Antonio says Father Pedro left the church around four p.m., telling him he was going home.'

'Then what...?'

Agente Serrano shrugged. 'Then nothing, Boss... until he was murdered.'

'That's the gap we need to fill.' Velázquez wrote more timelines with events on the whiteboard; then he pointed at what he'd just written: 'The gap in time between Father Pedro's leaving the Iglesia de Jesus del Gran Poder and the time he was killed.'

'Which was when exac'ly did we say again, Boss?' Javier Merino asked.

'We didn't... but the body was still warm, suggesting that

the murder had taken place no more than an hour before we arrived on the scene.'

'And you arrived at the flat shortly before eight,' Agente Pérez said. 'So we need to account for Father Pedro's movements between around four and sometime before eight p.m.'

'Exactly... those four hours.' Velázquez cleared his throat, then turned to Subinspector Gajardo. 'How did the two men get on playing golf together, José?'

'Father Pedro won, Boss...finished with a birdie by all accounts... Sounds like he's a pretty useful player—bloody amazing when you consider the man's age.'

'Might've been a motive for revenge,' Agent Serrano quipped.

Velázquez permitted himself a restrained grin. 'With sports psychology like that, Jorge, I can see I'd better not play you at pool.'

CHAPTER 4

Velázquez climbed into the Seat Ibiza and called Pe on his mobile, to tell her he would be home later than expected. But they had the de la Spadas coming over for dinner, Pe protested. Had he forgotten?

Velázquez hadn't forgotten. Juan de la Spada was one of the most successful bull-breeders in the business, while his wife was an up and coming actress, and the couple's comings and goings had recently become material for the gossip columns; but he found the prospect of having dinner with them no less boring for all that. Pe would be all right, because Laura de la Spada was cultured and capable of making conversation. Velázquez could picture the two women getting along like a house on fire, while he would be forced to listen to yet another lecture from Juan de la Spada on how he bred his bulls.

'It's just that there's been a murder, Pe—a particularly nasty and brutal one.'

'I said I'd be serving dinner at ten, so they should come over at nine-thirty,' she said. 'You'd better not let me down, Luis.'

'Okay, I'll be there… *Te quiero.*'

'I love you, too.'

Velázquez started up the engine and drove over to *Jorge's*, the bar that Pilar Ochoa had told him about. The place was full when he got there, and he had to squeeze between huddles of drinkers to get to the counter. He asked the barman, a muscled guy in a black T-shirt, if he knew a Ramón Ochoa. The barman shrugged, ran a hand over his shaved head. Loads of people came in this place, he said. And some of them were called Ramón. It was a fairly common name, after all, and customers didn't necessarily make a habit of telling everyone their surnames. 'People come here to relax,' he said. 'It's an informal kinda place, y'know?'

Velázquez took out the photograph the girl at the agency had given him and held it up for the man to see. 'This is him.'

The barman placed Velázquez's beer down on the counter, and looked at the photo before saying, 'Why do you ask?'

'I think his life may well be in serious danger.'

'You a cop?'

Velázquez nodded and flashed his ID.

'What kind of danger?'

'A friend of his has been murdered.'

The man's eyebrows rose. 'What friend would this be?'

'Look, I haven't got time to waste.'

'He was in here last night, as it happens.'

'He leave with anyone?'

The barman leaned over the counter and pointed: 'See the tall blond guy over by the wall there... one that's wearing far too much makeup, and an excuse for a dress?'

Velázquez nodded.

'Name's Clara... he knows Ramón, I think. Might try askin' him.'

Velázquez picked up his beer and crossed the bar, squeezing through the huddles of drinkers, a medley of leathers and shaved heads sporting peaked policeman's caps, Freddy Mercury moustaches, and drag. Velázquez made eye contact with the man the barman had pointed out. '*Hola*... you're Clara, I believe?' The man was wearing a skimpy red number, fishnet stockings, killer heels, and a blond wig and red lipstick; but despite all of the trouble he'd taken, he still just looked like a guy in a dress.

'That's right... and who might you be?'

Velázquez flashed his ID. Clara looked at it then shrugged. 'I haven't done anything... might be up for a little undercover work later though, honey, if you're in the mood to tango.'

'Always been more of a foxtrot man, I'm afraid.' Velázquez held up the photograph. 'I'm looking for this man... name's Ramón Ochoa. Somebody told me you know him.'

'I know all sorts of people, honey.'

'He was in this place last night.'

'What if he was?'

'I've reason to believe he could be in serious danger,' Velázquez said. 'Now did you see him here last night?'

Clara nodded.

'He leave with anybody?'

'English *chico* by the name of Eric Waters… skinny guy with short blond hair and far too many spots for my liking.'

'Know where this Eric Waters lives?'

'No, but he teaches at the Escuela de Idiomas.'

'How do you know where he works?'

'Me that introduced him to Ramón… I used to be one of his students.'

'That the school over on Avenida Doctor Fedriani?'

'You got it… doesn't shut till around nine, so if you go there now you might just catch him.'

'Thanks.'

' And don't forget to take a condom with you.'

'Huh?'

'Should always go prepared,' Clara said. ''Cause there's a nasty serial killer out there on the loose, case you hadn't heard.'

'You trying to tell me something?'

'AIDS, honey.'

Velázquez showed the young receptionist at the Escuela de Idiomas his ID, told her he needed to speak to an Eric Waters that taught there. 'Come with me,' she said.

The students were packing their things away as they entered the classroom. The receptionist told Waters he had a visitor, and Velázquez quickly introduced himself, holding up his ID as he did so.

Waters looked like a student himself, from the skinny frame and clothes—grey Levi's, blue Vans, plain white T-shirt—down to the fresh acne scars on his jaw and neck. 'It's about your friend

Ramón Ochoa… I think he may be in some kind of trouble and I want to help him.'

'Why? What's happened?'

'No time to explain… I need to find Ramón—any idea where he is?'

'I left him at my place before I came over here.' Eric spoke with an accent that was about as Spanish as the Hovis ad.

'Time was that?'

'I must've left home about twenty to six.'

'We're talking p.m., are we?'

'That's right.'

'When did Ramón show at your place?'

'Not very long before I left.'

'How long before?'

'Maybe ten, fifteen minutes.'

'So why'd he stay there if you were leaving?'

'He'd spent the night at mine, then left in the morning and couldn't find his mobile, reckoned he probably left it behind.'

'He find it?'

Eric shrugged his narrow shoulders. 'Still looking for it when I left.'

'Think there's any chance he's still there?'

'Guess that depends on whether or not he's found it.'

'You going there now?'

'No, I've got to teach a private lesson after I leave this place, and then I'm going to meet some friends.'

'What's your address?'

'Number twenty Calle Correduría, flat 3B.'

Velázquez made a note of it before he said, 'What sort of mood was Ramón in when you left him?'

'Seemed pretty agitated.'

'Any idea why that might've been?'

'How'd feel in his shoes?'

'Huh…?'

'It was an expensive one.'

Velázquez parked in one of the side streets off the Alameda de Hercules, then went in search of Calle Correduría. But he couldn't find the street, so he asked an old man for directions. The man pointed with his walking stick: it was just the other side of the Alameda. Velázquez thanked the man, and set off across the muddy stretch of rubble-strewn waste land that took its name from the pairs of tall twin pillars at either end that were dedicated to Hercules. A girl wearing a tatty handkerchief for a skirt came over and asked him if he'd like to have some fun. He glanced at her without slackening his pace, and the girl did her best to crack an appealing smile so that Velázquez caught sight of the orthodontic nightmare she had for teeth. Velázquez told her he was a '*poli*' and the girl said in that case he could have it for half price. 'Sure you could charge it to your expense account, darlin'.'

He pressed on and soon found himself on Correduria, one of the side streets that run from the Alameda up to Calle Feria. The building was up near the next corner, a tall, nondescript affair from the outside. Velázquez pushed a random buzzer on the console, and somebody buzzed him in without bothering to ask who was calling.

There was no lift, so he ran up the stairs and found the door. It had been left ajar. He knocked on the panelled wood, but nobody came. He tried the buzzer. Still no sign of anybody, so he entered the flat.

It was dark and there was some kind of crazy music playing. Flamenco meets Sid Vicious. In a dark alley. '*Hola?*' Velázquez called out. 'Is anybody home?'

Nobody answered.

Velázquez flicked the light switch.

Nothing happened.

Then something, or some*body*, hit him on the back of the head...

Pe was in the kitchen, doing the dishes, when Velázquez finally got home at just after three a.m., and she gave him a look that would have stopped a bull in its tracks. You were to describe her, first thing you'd probably say is that she was drop-dead gorgeous. Second thing would probably be that she didn't look like your average bullfighter. You'd comment on her figure: the way her black leggings and red T-shirt were clingy enough to make the laziest schoolboy want to study her geometry. 'Nice of you to show at last,' she said. 'Little late for dinner, though.'

'I can explain, Pe.'

'Always can... that's half the problem.'

'You don't know what happened.'

'No.' She sighed and her beautiful black eyes flashed. 'But I'm sure it'll make a good story.' She looked at him, hands on hips, every molecule in her body somehow working to show just how *pissed off* she was. 'Come on,' she said. 'Shock me... tell me how you threw the house through the window to make sure you'd get here on time, even though you still didn't make it. What was it this time? Don't tell me. Some psycho of a gangster turned his pet Komodo dragon loose on you... One lash of its tongue'd be enough to kill a man forty times over. So you jumped on its back and wrestled with it, until you finally killed it and then came rushing home to your blushing damsel of a bullfighter girlfriend, to boast... Am I right?'

'Not quite.'

'Maybe it was a pet crocodile, then... or better still, a pool full of piranha fish? Four seconds in the water and there'd've been nothing left of you but your shoe laces.'

'You're forgetting something, Pe.'

'What...?'

'I'm wearing slip-ons.'

The following morning, Velázquez sipped the coffee—if that wasn't too grand a word—from the machine downstairs, then put the plastic cup down on his desk and gave it a look of bitter disapproval before dialling the number for the Escuela de

Idiomas. A pleasant female voice answered. Velázquez explained who he was and asked to speak to Eric Waters. 'It's urgent,' he said.

'I'm sorry, but Eric phoned in sick today.'

'*Gracias.*' Velázquez hung up and headed out of the office, stopping at the door only to tell the members of his team he needed them out knocking on doors again. 'And remember to keep records of who you've spoken to.'

'All I need,' Merino said, sounding like he was distinctly peed-off.

'Don't tell me you'd prefer to be doing the rounds of the gay bars again, Javi?'

'This what I get for bringing you your coffee in the morning, Boss?'

'That what you call it?' Velázquez turned and went out, took the lift down to the basement car park, found his car and set off for Eric Waters' place. Pulled up minutes later, on Calle Correduría, and stepped out onto the cobbled street.

He hadn't walked more than a few metres before a dealer came up to him: tall skinny character in jeans, white vest, shades, scimitar-shaped sideburns. 'Need a wrap?' Velázquez was about to tell the man he was a '*poli*'; but then he had another idea: 'I'll take a couple.' The coast was clear—he'd checked. 'Ten thousand *pesetas*.' Velázquez tried to knock him down, but the bastard laughed in his face.

Just then, a squad car turned the corner, and Velázquez felt his heart thumping in his chest. 'Okay,' he said. 'But quick about it—here come the *polis*.'

The exchange was made just before the squad car drew up. The uniform sitting in the passenger seat looked out at Velázquez, who told the man who he was and flashed his ID. 'Informant of mine,' he said, and the uniform nodded as if to show he understood, then the car went on its way.

Velázquez breathed a sigh of relief. He was an idiot to go buying heroin in the street like that. Especially round here. The

Alamada de Hercules was a magnet for cops, after all. Far safer to go out to the Tres Mil to buy the stuff: police rarely went there, unless they were on a raid; and then they'd go in large numbers.

Velázquez went back to Eric Waters' place, and pushed a button on the console at random. A woman's voice asked him who he was. Velázquez told her he'd come to fix the plumbing.

'Nothing wrong with my plumbing,' the woman said.

'No, it's on the floor below... sorry, I pushed the wrong button.'

The woman buzzed him in. Not wanting to go through a repeat of his last visit, Velázquez took his gun out as he ran up the stairs, slowing down as he reached the third floor.

This time the door was locked. He pushed the buzzer. Nothing. He pushed it again.

Nobody was in.

Or if they were, then they weren't in a very sociable mood.

Velázquez took out his lock picks and got the door open, then entered the flat, holding his gun out in front of him. He found the light switch and pressed it. Nothing happened. Then he noticed the television was on over in the corner of the room. On the screen, a blond man was fellating another man. The sound was turned off.

Glancing up at the ceiling, Velázquez noticed there was no bulb. Perhaps Ramón took it out, to give himself the advantage in the event of a surprise visit. The shutters were partially drawn and the light that filtered in, combined with that from the television, was just enough for Velázquez to be able to see by.

He moved forward into the room, keeping his gun up in front of him, knees bent, crouching like a hunter stalking his prey. A short hallway led off the living room, and there were three doors in it. He kicked the first one open, and found himself staring at a toilet and a sink.

Nobody there.

He kicked the door to his right, then took a quick look in.

There was a double bed, unmade, with nobody in it. That just left the second door on the left.

Velázquez kicked that open too: a bathtub that doubled up as a shower. He tore the screen back.

Nobody there.

CHAPTER 5

Velázquez called in to *Jorge's* early in the afternoon. To his surprise, the place seemed to be doing a fairly good trade, despite the hour. No sooner had he got to the counter than Clara came over to him: 'Hello, sailor.'

'I'm not a sailor, I'm a *poli*.'

'Every guy in this place is a sailor, far as I'm concerned, hon.'

Velázquez smiled and said, 'Whatever floats your boat.' He turned to the barman: 'I'll have a beer. And whatever Clara wants.'

'Better not say what I really *really* want, hon, because it's dirty, but I'll settle for a large glass of Chablis.' Clara dug into his golden handbag and brought out a packet of Camels. He took a cigarette from the pack and lit up, had himself a long drag that looked like it hurt, and exhaled twin columns of smoke through his large nostrils, before offering Velázquez the pack.

Velazquez declined with a shake of the head. 'I gave up.'

'I like a man with will power.'

Velázquez let that one go hurtling by and said, 'I'm still looking for Ramón Ochoa.'

Clara sipped his Chablis. 'Sound like you got it bad, hon, and that ain't good.' He took another agonized drag on his Camel. 'What's this Ramón got that I haven't?'

'Information.'

'You should check out the mine of info I got down my knickers, hon.'

The door opened, and Eric Waters stepped in with another man. Clara said, 'Talk of the devil–there they are… Seems like it could be your lucky day.'

Velázquez hadn't recognized Ochoa: face seemed longer than

in the mug shot, and it looked like someone had left the man's nose wondering which way was north. Had his hair tied back in a ponytail—another new touch—and could have done with a shave or two.

The pair made their way over to the counter, and Velázquez went and joined them. 'Hi Eric,' he said. 'Who's your friend?'

Ramón Ochoa said, 'Who's asking?'

Velázquez took out his ID and flashed it. 'I've been looking for you.'

Ochoa's brown eyes were full of bitter derision. 'Well I sure ain't been looking for you.'

'We need to talk.'

'You might, but I'm here to have a drink.'

'I'm not sure I like your manners.'

'Weren't meant to.'

Just then, the barman placed Ramón's beer down on the counter. He picked it up and took a sip, then leered at Velázquez and belched in his face.

'You can either come down to the *Jefatura* with me now, of your own accord, Ramón,' Velázquez said, 'or I can arrest you.'

'What you gonna arrest me on?'

'Suspicion of murder.'

'*What*…? You kidding me?'

'Afraid not.'

'Who the fuck'm I suppose to've killed?'

'Father Pedro Mora.'

Ramón threw his drink in Velázquez's face, then turned and made a dash for it. Velázquez gave chase, but tripped over an outstretched foot; by the time he got outside there was no sign of Ramón.

Velázquez called Agente Serrano and explained what had just happened. 'I need you to go over to Ramón Ochoa's mother's place and see if he's there.'

'Sure. You got an address, Boss?'

Velázquez read it out to him from his notebook.

'And what if he's not there?'

'Scour every gay bar in the city,' Velázquez said. 'Talk to people, see if you can find anyone who knows him and might've seen him. Take Merino and Pérez with you.'

'I could use a copy of the mug shot, Boss.'

'Ask Subinspector Gajardo to get you a copy... And contact me straightaway if you find him.'

They hung up and Velázquez went over to the Escuela de Idiomas, where he pulled Eric Waters out of a lesson and asked him if he had any idea where his friend Ramón Ochoa might be. Eric Waters shrugged. 'How should I know? I mean, we're not married—'

'If you see him, can I trust you to call me?'

'Yes, of course,' Waters said. 'Now if that's all, I hope you won't mind if I go back to my class. They've got an exam next Wednesday and half of them still know as much about the Perfect tenses as I do about a nun's—'

'Please pass on my apologies to your students, will you,' Velázquez said, turning to leave. 'You might also tell them that I managed to pass my exams in English, and I don't know the first thing about nuns, either.'

As he drove through the streets, Velázquez took out his mobile and called Serrano. 'What's new?'

'Talking to the guy's mother at her flat right now.'

'And...?'

'Says she hasn't seen or heard from him in days.'

'Tell Merino to stay on watch outside the front door to the block in his car, and you and Pérez can carry on looking for him.'

'Right you are, Boss.'

Velázquez was feeling awful again by now. He needed a fix, but he could hardly shoot up in the street; so he headed back to his flat. And when he got in, he was relieved to find that Pe wasn't at home. That meant he could shoot up in the kitchen without fear of discovery.

He took a minute or two to relish the experience, before he hid the baggie in its usual hiding place. Then he went back out in search of Ramón Ochoa.

He spent the rest of the afternoon and evening getting nowhere fast. Called the other officers in his team just after ten, only to learn they hadn't managed to turn up anything useful either.

One of those days.

Velázquez had that awful all-wound-up-and-nowhere-to-go feeling he often got at the end of days like this, when nothing seemed to be going right on a case. Sort of day a *matador* must have when he comes up against a bull he just can't work with.

Pe was sitting on the sofa reading a novel when Velázquez got in, just after midnight. She looked at him and said, 'Have a good day?'

'Not exactly.'

'How come?'

Velázquez made straight for the drinks cabinet. 'Fancy joining me in one?'

'Was your day *that* bad?' Pe asked him. When she didn't get an answer, she shrugged and said, 'Go on, then. Put a dash of water in mine.'

He came over with the drinks and sat next to her on the leather sofa. Pe took hers and they clinked glasses. 'Your health,' Velázquez said and took a sip of his Scotch.

'*Salud!*' replied Pe, as she put her book down on the coffee table.

Velázquez glanced at the cover: *Libra* by Don DeLillo. 'Any good?' he asked. She nodded. 'It's about Lee Harvey Oswald and the assassination of JFK.'

Trust Pe to read about something like that, Velázquez

thought. The police balls-up to end all police balls-ups. He picked the book up and read the blurb on the back cover. 'Sounds interesting,' he said, and put it back down. Then sighed and kicked off his loafers. 'What sort of a day have you had, Pe?'

'I went out to the ranch and practised.'

'Of course, you're out at Antequera tomorrow evening, aren't you?'

Pe nodded and said, 'Just hope they give me some decent bulls to work with.'

Velázquez tapped twice on the pinewood coffee table.

Pe laughed. 'For a cop you're not half superstitious.'

'What's being a cop got to do with it?'

'Cops are supposed to be methodical and rational, aren't they?'

Velázquez shrugged. 'All I know is we're supposed to catch the bad guys.' He watched Pe run a hand through her long mane of wavy black hair and marvelled again that this woman fought bulls.

Sensing his admiration, she smiled and said, 'So are you going to tell me about your day or not, then, Luis?'

'I finally caught up with the murder suspect and then let him get away.'

'You sure he's the killer?'

'No.'

'Maybe it's not such a bad thing that he got away, then.'

'That's what I love about you, Pe.'

'What…?'

'The way you can take a twenty-four carat cock-up I've made and put a positive spin on it.'

They fell silent and sat gazing into each other's eyes, then Pe said, 'That the only thing?'

Afterwards, they sat sipping their drinks as they watched the news, pacified by the release of the storm cloud of hot febrile passion that had built up between them. There was a report on

41

the rising unemployment figures; then they listened to a report on the murder of Father Pedro Mora. 'So far the police have made no arrests,' the newscaster said. Velázquez picked up the control unit and posted the newscaster into orbit.

'Let's go to bed,' he said.

He fell asleep as soon as his head hit the pillow, and slipped straight into an old recurring nightmare. He was in a car park, and there was nobody else about... or at least, so he'd thought, until he climbed into his beloved old Alfa Romeo—and somebody hit him from behind. When he came round, he found that his knees were pushing up in his chest and his hands were tied. He tried to shout but there was a gag in his mouth.

His heart was hammering in his ears.

He was terrified.

I'm in the boot of a car, he thought. And it's moving.

He wondered where he was being taken.

He remembered how it was he'd got here.

A man had called him on his mobile, and told him to go and get into his car. Said he'd come and find him.

He knew where I'd parked, Velázquez thought. He must have been watching me. My own stupid fault, he told himself. Should've been more careful.

Probably the same guy who hit me on the back of the head that time over at Eric Waters' place, he thought. Could be what the guy'd been referring to, talking on the phone, when he said our paths had crossed before one time but he didn't get the chance to introduce himself...

What's he tied me up for?

He said he wanted to talk.

Maybe he does.

What about?

Just try to stay calm and you might find out, Velázquez told himself.

That was good advice. *Try and stay calm.*

Yeah, just try and take it sometime when you're tied up in

the boot of a car.

Just try and take it.

Better than the alternative, though.

What alternative?

There wasn't any alternative.

Precisely.

Where is this guy taking me?

You already wondered about that, and you didn't come up with an answer the first time.

Keep thinking. That's the ticket. Keep those thoughts coming.

This guy wants to talk to you.

That's it. What about?

Who is he?

No idea.

Think of this as a learning experience.

That's it, think of life as a learning curve. Shit happens, but you can learn from it.

Yeah…

My back's hurting like hell.

Soon you'll be out of here. Just hold on.

That's it. Just hold on.

Try not to piss your pants.

That's rule number one.

Good rule in a crisis.

Should put that one in the police handbook.

The car stopped.

We're here.

Wherever the fuck *here* is.

Soon find out.

He heard the sound of the car door slamming shut.

Footsteps on gravel.

The boot being opened.

'Time to go, mister.'

Velázquez felt himself being lifted out of the boot, and the next moment he landed on his feet. It was very quiet, and there was a smell of horse manure. Somewhere out in the sticks, Velázquez thought; then somebody pushed him in the back, and he was marched into a building.

He heard doors opening and closing, wooden boards having replaced gravel underfoot.

He was pushed into a chair.

He tried to get up but something hit him and he felt a searing pain in his head and saw stars. Then he must have passed out, and when he came round he was strapped to the chair by his ankles and wrists.

He tried to free himself, but it was useless.

'What's this all about?' he shouted. And was surprised to hear his own voice. At least the bastard had taken the gag out.

'You should calm down, Inspector Jefe. No point in getting yourself all worked up.' Somewhere in his dream, a part of Velázquez was aware that he was dreaming, reliving an experienced he'd lived through. That part of him knew it was Bill and the Black Lady who'd taken him. Well, they couldn't both have been lying under the back seat of his Alfa Romeo; that would have been Bill. But the Black Lady would show later... then they'd start to pump him full of heroin.

But what was it all about?

'Who are you?' he heard himself saying in his dream. 'What do you want?'

'I'm afraid that's what you might call privileged information.'

He heard sirens and figured his luck was in, then the sirens developed an odd tendency to ring. *What the...* He opened his eyes. His bedside telephone was ringing.

He reached out with a fumbling hand, and picked it up. '*Hola?*'

'Velázquez? Comisario Alonso here... another body's turned up. Fucking city's turning into an abattoir.'

'You got an address, Comisario?' Velázquez said, reaching for the notepad and pen he always kept handy by the phone.

Comisario Alonso told him the address and he wrote it down.

'Just had the mayor on the phone,' the Comisario said. 'Been chewing my ear off about the damage to the tourist trade... Almost choked on the amount of smoke was coming down the line. *Joder!* You got any idea how much money these murders could cost this city, if we can't catch the killer quickly, Velázquez?'

'You want me on this case, Comisario? Or d'you want me to do the PR for the Tourist Board?' Velázquez felt like saying.

But somehow he managed to bite his tongue.

CHAPTER 6

The frogmen had already got the body out of the river by the time Velázquez arrived on the scene, and somebody had checked through the victim's pockets. A wallet had been found. Velázquez looked through it and found various cards, including the victim's *carné*.

He halted the progress of two ambulance men carrying the body on a stretcher, and pulled back the sheet. Another dog collar. The body was on its side, so that Velázquez could see the face in profile. It was familiar to him. A kitchen knife of the kind that had been used on Father Pedro Mora was sticking out of the victim's backside.

The Inspector Jefe dropped the sheet, and allowed the ambulance men to go on their way, then asked the uniform who had given him the wallet if he knew who discovered the body. 'Nightshift worker on his way home,' the officer said. 'Saw it floating on the water as he was crossing the bridge.'

At that moment Gajardo came hurrying over. 'Another priest, is it, Boss?'

Velázquez nodded. 'Name of Father Aloysius.'

'Who identified him?'

'Vic had his wallet in his pocket with his *carné* in it,' Velázquez said. 'Although I recognized the man's face, as a matter of fact.'

'Oh…?'

'Talked to him when I called over at the Iglesia de Jesus del Gran Poder about Father Mora… two men were friends.'

'At least we know who he is, then,' Gajardo said. 'That's a start… seems like we're up against someone with a grudge against priests, Boss.'

'Looks like it.'

'Serial killer, do you think?'

'Little too early to say. But the *modus operandi* seems to've been the same as the one used on Father Pedro.'

'The bullet and the kitchen knife, Boss?'

'Dunno about whether he was shot, but a kitchen knife was definitely used.'

'Nasty.'

'And some.'

Velázquez turned and saw the stocky form of Gómez, approaching. He acknowledged him with a nod of the head and said, 'I'll need you to check and see if this one was shot the same way as Father Pedro, of course, Juan. And if so, then we'll need Ballistics to run tests to see if the same sort of bullet was used.'

'I were a betting man,' Gajardo cut in, 'I'd lay my mother-in-law's bloomers that you'll find the same kind of bullet in this one.'

Gómez looked at Velázquez and jerked his thumb in Gajardo's general direction. 'Way your number two's going, Luis, he'll soon be a very rich man.'

'Either that or his mother-in-law's gonna feel the draft a lot more this winter,' Velázquez said. 'Don't suppose there's a chance of any DNA?'

'Not with the vic being in the river.' The *Médico Forense* turned his head in time to see the ambulance set off. 'Dunno what's got into this city,' he said. 'Priests never used to get brutally murdered.'

'Did back in the Civil War... and often they were castrated first.'

'But that's different, Luis... It was politics.'

'I wonder if they would agree.'

Gómez brought out a packet of Camels, took one from the pack and lit up.

Velázquez flashed him a sideways look. 'Thought you packed up?'

Gómez took a long drag, then exhaled. 'I did.'

'Nothing like will power.'

'So they tell me.'

Velázquez heard someone coming up behind him. He turned and found himself looking at Judge Montero. 'What've we got, Inspector Jefe?'

Velázquez quickly brought him up to speed.

'What do you want me to do now, Boss?' Subinspector Gajardo asked.

'Not much you can do here.' A quick glance at his Swatch told Velázquez that it was coming up to five a.m. 'I were you, I'd go home'n grab a little kip. See you at the *Jefatura* first thing in the morning.'

'Okay. *Buenas noches.*'

Velázquez remained at the crime scene for a while, talking to the *Médico Forense*; then he drove back to the *Jefatura*, left the car in the basement car park and went to a bar that opened early—or stayed open late—on Blas Infante. Had the waiter bring him *café con leche* in a glass and a croissant. He knew from Pe that Balzac, one of her favourite authors, wrote at night and drank coffee from pint mugs to keep himself going. Ended up dying of caffeine poisoning, or so they said.

Could you really die from caffeine poisoning? he wondered. There was one for his friend, Juan Gómez, the *Médico Forense*. He'd know about that. But how did they manage to ascertain the cause of death, seeing as Balzac had died somewhere around the middle of the nineteenth century? Had they really been able to work out that sort of thing so long ago?

Velázquez smiled at the waywardness of his own thoughts and took another sip of his coffee. Pe would say he was parading his working-class roots having it in a glass. Truth was, he just preferred it that way.

He had the waiter bring him a glass of brandy, then poured it into his coffee to make a *carajillo*. It tasted good and woke him up a little. He paid the bill, then went into the *Jefatura* and took the lift up to his office. Given the hour, he'd expected to have the place to himself; but no sooner had he sat at his desk than his telephone rang. He snatched it up. '*Hola?*'

'Comisario Alonso here. What do you know about this second vic?'

'Another elderly priest, Boss… name was Father Aloysius, and he served at the same church as the other priest that was murdered… They were friends.'

'How was he killed?'

'Same *modus operandi* as with Father Pedro by the look of it… Kitchen knife was used on him in the same manner, although we're still waiting for confirmation that the vic was shot.'

'So we're looking for a serial killer with a thing about priests and an imagination like Goya's.'

'Must be one seriously fucked-up individual, Comisario.'

'Keep me updated, okay?'

Gómez looked up from the body laid out on the dissecting table as Velázquez entered the lab. 'Hi, Luis,' Gómez said, 'you look terrible.'

'Thanks, *amigo*.'

'No, seriously, I mean it… I didn't notice it earlier, when we were down by the river, but you look like you haven't slept in a month.'

Velázquez shrugged, thinking Gómez looked pretty knackered, too. 'Anything new that you can tell me?'

'Found a bullet.'

'Same place as with the first vic?'

Gómez nodded. 'Got it in one.'

'Need Ballistics to compare it with the bullet taken from Father Pedro Mora.'

'Already sent it over.'

'Can see you've been busy this morning, Juan.'

'You know me, Luis.' The *Médico Forense* picked up a clipboard and looked at the report that was attached to it. 'Body temperature of the second priest doesn't tell us much, of course, because—'

'Body was found in the river, so it would've been affected by the temperature of the water.'

'Exactly... And there's no DNA, either...' Gómez took off his gloves. 'Trouble with bodies that show up in water, I'm afraid. Evidence all tends to get washed away. Still, at least we've got the bullet to be thankful for.'

Perhaps the killer knew that, Velázquez thought. It was interesting, because the *modus operandi* suggested the frenzied attack of a lunatic; and yet the fact that the killer had dumped the body in the river seemed to contradict this. Perhaps that's all part of his plan, Velázquez thought. Perhaps we're dealing with a cool customer that wants to make us think he's a lunatic who kills in a mad frenzy, to throw us off the scent...

'Had breakfast yet, Luis?'

Velázquez nodded. 'Stopped off in a cafe before I came here.'

'Going for mine now.' Gómez hung up his lab coat. 'I'll walk down with you,' he said, and they went out through the swing doors.

While they waited for the lift, Gómez asked Velázquez how things were going with Pe. 'Just great,' he replied.

'You're that rare beast, Luis—a cop who's happily in love.'

The doors opened, and they stepped inside. It was empty, and Gómez pushed the button for the ground floor. The lift began to descend and Velázquez said, 'She's just about perfect... I mean, she's beautiful, honest, loyal, intelligent, and she's a great cook... I really don't know what a girl like her sees in a guy like me. I mean, she could have anyone she wants.'

'Carry on like that and you'll make me hate you.' Gómez smiled. 'Tell me she's got bad breath... tell me she doesn't look so great after she takes her false teeth out at night.'

Velázquez laughed. 'Don't think we don't have our ups and downs like any other couple.'

'That's better... tell me more of that stuff. Tell me you argue like hell and scratch each other's eyes out.'

'We only ever argue about one thing,' Velázquez said.

'And what's that?'

'Well, if you can believe it, Pe's decided she wants to be a bullfighter.'

'But she can't!'

'There've been a few female bullfighters over the past twenty years or so, as a matter of fact.'

'You don't need to tell *me* that… but even so it's no life for an intelligent young woman like Pe.'

'Try telling *her* that.'

The lift came to a stop, and they stepped out and headed through the small lobby.

'Always thought most women hate bullfighting,' Gómez said. 'From what I read in the newspapers nowadays, anyway, about how they're trying to ban it up in Catalonia—all the animal rights people… Lot of guys involved in it, too.'

'Pe supports animal rights big time.'

'But how can she if she wants to be a *torera*?'

'Says the bull doesn't feel it so much because it gets the chance to fight back,' Velázquez said. 'Like when you're in a fight and a guy hits you but you don't feel it much because you're too busy hitting him, or trying to, you know?'

They left the building and crossed the road. The sun had just come up, but there was hardly anyone out on the street.

'Can't remember the last time I was in a fight, Luis, to be honest.'

'Difference, the way she sees it, between hitting a man who's free to hit you back and hitting a man who's tied up in a chair.'

'What is…?'

'Bullfighting's the former, the way she sees it.'

'So what's the latter?'

'All this animal testing they do to make cosmetic products and farm rearing animals just so they can be slaughtered. Like they do with livestock and poultry, battery hen eggs and salmon and tuna… Pe's dead against all that. Way she sees it, the people who're trying to ban bullfighting are barking up the wrong tree. She says it's about having an old-fashioned world view in which man—or woman, in her case—is just another living creature on a level footing with the rest of the natural world.'

'Instead of one who thinks he can lord it over the rest of creation, you mean?'

'Exactly.'

Gómez flashed Velázquez a sideways glance. 'What do you think, Luis?'

'I'm dead against animal testing, too. Like Pe. But I eat meat, and so does she. For me, it's a question of accepting the reality of the natural world and not wanting to live in some modern plasticky substitute.'

'No, about bullfighting, I mean…?'

'One part of me thinks it's cruel, sure… but on the other hand, nature's cruel and some people just don't want to admit it.'

'Sounds as though you're like me… Love to see a good *corrida* but can't find any good moral justification for it.'

Velázquez wasn't quite sure he did feel that way about it, but it was all too complex and difficult to explain and he didn't have the time right now. Bullfighting was an important part of his life. He'd been watching the *corridas* since he was a small kid and he couldn't imagine a world without them. They were an essential part of Spain's cultural identity; part and parcel of his own identity, too, even if he didn't always like to admit it. Why, he even thought like a *torero* at times, and approached his cases like one.

'Nobody ever said murder's right either's another way to look at it, Juan,' Velázquez said. 'But you and I'd both be out of a job if there weren't any killers out there.'

They walked in silence a little way, then Gómez said, 'Pe ever given it a go?'

'She's signed up for the whole season, so she tells me… Fact, she's appearing in a *corrida* this evening at a small bullring out on the way to Antequera,' Velázquez said. 'I tried to talk her out of it, but she won't listen to reason.' He sighed. '*Joder*, I'd be only too happy to see Pe going out to work... I mean, I'm not one of these old-fashioned macho types who wants his woman to stay at home. Not at all. I've tried suggesting that she train to do something... something...'

'... Normal...?'

'Exactly... I'd support her all the way if she wanted to become a teacher or a lawyer or a dentist, or'—Velázquez waved his hand in frustration—'whatever. But a *bullfighter*...?'

'Maybe she'll go off the idea.'

'I sure as hell hope so,' Velázquez said. 'Don't suppose you'd fancy coming out to watch her with me later?'

'Sure, I'd love to.'

'Pick you up here some time close after four, then.'

'Right.' Gómez smiled. 'Pe must be a brave girl.

'She's that all right.' Velázquez stopped next to the Seat Ibiza parked at the curb. 'Just wish she was a bit more of a coward, like me.'

Velázquez headed for home, and checked in on Pe as soon as he got back to see if she was up. No, it was okay: she was still sound asleep; so he went out into the kitchen and shot up. Then he went drove back over to the *Jefatura*. Serrano and Merino were already at their desks. 'What I like to see,' he said. 'Homicide officers working hard bright and early.'

'Reports to write, boss,' Merino groaned without looking up.

'Has to be done, Javier,' Velázquez said, as he booted up his computer. 'Important part of the job.' He sighed. 'There's been another murder. A priest. Body was found in the river in the night... served at the same church over on the Plaza de San Lorenzo.'

Jorge Serrano sat up in his chair. 'Could be a serial killer we're after then...'

'One who's got a serious grudge against priests if it is,' said Gajardo, who had just come breezing in. Despite not having slept much, he was looking as spruce and dapper as ever in his blue pinstripe; his hair was so loaded with gel it shone like a mackerel, and you could see the tracks where the comb had passed, while his black lace-ups would serve as a shaving mirror in an emergency. Velázquez wondered how his number two managed to look so fresh and immaculate at all times, whatever the conditions, even though his marriage was supposed to be on the rocks. But then, the man's not grappling with a heroin habit like I am, Velázquez thought.

Agente Pérez said, 'Seems quite a coincidence that he should've served at the same church as Father Pedro, Boss, don't you think?'

'Or maybe it's not at all,' Javier Merino suggested.

'Exactly what I was thinking,' Sara Pérez concurred. Then she got up from her desk, carrying yesterday's *El Sur* in her hand, which she tossed onto Velazquez's desk. 'Thought you might want to read this, Boss.'

'What is it?'

'Woman writing a book about Father Pedro—gave an interview about it.'

Velázquez saw the headline: BOOK ABOUT MURDERED PRIEST. He quickly read the article, then looked up at Sara Pérez. 'So the woman's not written the book yet?'

'No, she's working on it now… Journalist who works for the newspaper is a friend of mine and put me wise to her, Boss.'

'You spoken to the woman yet?'

'Called her a few minutes ago.'

'And…?'

'Claims to've had an affair with Father Pedro Mora.'

'This before he became a priest?'

'That's right—way back in nineteen thirty six, on Tenerife… Says he wanted to marry her.' Pérez's lips curved up in a wry smile. 'Although the affair would've been platonic I should imagine, given the time.'

'No suggestion of his being gay, then?'

'Not so far as I can make out,' Pérez replied. 'Apparently she's going to write about their affair and why he went into the priesthood.'

'Good work, Sara.'

'There's more, Boss... The writer sent her manuscript—what she's written of it so far—to the journalist that called me. Anyway, my friend's just called and asked me if I'd like her to run off a copy, so I'll go over and pick it up now if you'd like to read it?'

'I sure would.'

As he watched Agente Pérez leave the office, Velázquez understood how it was that other men got tongue tied around her. Not that he was similarly afflicted himself. He liked Sara Pérez. Liked and respected her, and was glad to have her in his department—not because she was immoderately attractive, but because she showed all of the signs of becoming a damned good cop.

CHAPTER 7

Two hours later, Velázquez was sitting at his desk reading the unfinished manuscript. Seemed a fairly run of the mill love story, only set in 1936, with the Civil War bubbling in the background: boy Pedro meets girl Anna. Pedro makes a play, Anna cuts him off. Pedro threatens to go and do something desperate... *'I swear, if I can't have you, then I'll assassinate somebody, or run away and become a priest.'*

Velázquez turned to the end of the chapter; there was a rather touching episode about the young Anna Segura...

Ordinarily Father never brought his work home. Even so, I had heard him let slip a few comments to my mother about the possibility of an uprising against the Government in Madrid.

This particular afternoon Father seemed quite distraught when he got back, and disappeared into his study. Mother went in to ask if he needed anything, and happened to leave the door ajar. Well, I was nothing if not curious, as you can imagine, so I loitered outside with my school books for a moment. Then an idea occurred to me, and I put my books on the floor and got down on my knees: if Mother were to come out of the room of a sudden, I would just gather my books as though I had dropped them and go on my way.

So there I was, outside the room, eavesdropping, when I heard Father say that a terrible thing had happened. General Balmes had been trying out a pistol at the shooting range, when a young man in soldier's uniform burst in, brought out a gun and shot him dead. My father, who had been alone with the General at the time, had given chase but the lad got away... Father was clearly quite at a loss as to why the young man should have shot the General, or who he was working for—unless perhaps it was for General Franco ... "But the truly awful thing is," I heard Father say, 'the assassin was none other than that young Pedro chap who's been courting

Anna…' I heard them agree to keep it from me for my sake. Father said: 'Not a word about any of what I've just told you to a living soul.' 'Quite right, Paco,' Mother assented, 'and we must of course make sure he never comes near her again.'

Moments later, I heard footsteps, and Mother emerged from the room. She was clearly affected by the news, because she passed me without saying a word as I knelt and gathered my books. In fact, I don't think she even noticed I was there.

Needless to say, I never saw Pedro again after that. Years passed and the episode with Pedro came to seem little more than a very minor footnote in my life; and now my memories of Pedro are just that—memories… and rather old and dusty ones at that.

I was nevertheless intrigued when I first read in a history book something that gave me cause to believe Pedro—the silly and hopelessly romantic young fool who had courted me—played a vital role in Spanish history.

You see, General Balmes's 'suicide' gave General Franco the pretext he needed to travel over to Las Palmas, to preside over the funeral. And from there Franco was able to coordinate his Rebel Army's attack on mainland Spain of the following day that kicked off the Civil War. 'I swear, if I can't have you then I'll assassinate somebody, or run away and become a priest,' Pedro had said.

In rejecting him as I did, was I somehow responsible for transforming Pedro from lover to murderer?

I suppose the real question is, would the Civil War have been averted had I relented and gone on a date with Pedro that evening? Did millions die simply because I rejected him?

The next chapter switched to Pedro, and the narrative described the taking of the villages of El Real de la Jara, Monesterio, Llerena, Zafra and Los Lobos de Marmona, by Franco's troops, leaving blood and slaughter behind them before finally taking Almendralejo. The Fascists took one thousand prisoners, a hundred of them women. And the young Pedro seemed to relish in particular his part in firing upon the citizens of Almendralejo, until there was not a single one of them left standing…

Some man of God, Velázquez thought in disgust, and it occurred to him that the episodes he'd been reading about might well have some bearing on Father Pedro's murder…

At this point Velázquez figured he needed to talk to the author; so he got up and made to leave the office. As he opened the door, Gajardo called over to him.

'Gonna talk to Anna Segura.' Velazquez tapped the manuscript.

'Mind if I come with you?'

'Be my guest.'

They took Velázquez's car, and arrived at the author's home in the Old Quarter, on Pérez Galdos, at just after three. The building was an elegant affair with louvered windows. Anna Segura buzzed them in and was waiting in the doorway when they stepped out of the lift onto the landing of the third floor.

At a glance, Velázquez reckoned she must be around seventy-five, even though she was rather jazzily dressed in black leggings, pink T-shirt and ballet pumps. '*Buenos tardes.* I'm the Inspector Jefe del Grupo de Homicidios,' he said, holding his ID out for her to see. 'And this is my colleague, Subinspector Gajardo.'

'*Buenas tardes*… How can I help you?'

Close up, Velázquez realized she'd had a number of facelifts, and, seeing how much makeup she was wearing, added five or maybe ten years to his original estimate. 'I'm interested in your manuscript,' he said. 'Would you mind if I asked you one or two questions about it?'

'Come on in.' Anna Segura stepped back and opened the door wider. They stepped inside and found themselves in the living room. Place was done out with polished parquet flooring and a mixture of oil paintings and black-and-white photographs hanging on the white-washed walls; the oils were landscapes, the photographs street-scenes.

'Please take a seat, gentlemen.' She gestured towards the

floral cotton sofa and sat in one of the matching chairs, over by the window. The sun was streaming in, so that Velázquez had to use his hand as a visor. 'I'm sorry,' Anna Segura said, 'the sun's a nuisance.' She got up and adjusted the slats on the Venetian blind. 'That's better.'

Once Anna Segura had returned to her chair, she gave the Inspector Jefe a thin smile. 'So... you wanted to talk about my manuscript... Have you read it?'

'Yes, some of it... I was just wondering if it's true that you knew Father Pedro Mora when he was younger?'

'Oh yes, absolutely... the Pedro in my story is the one who was murdered, sadly... And I did know him very well, yes.'

'From your manuscript it appears that he was very much in love with you.'

'Yes, he was... which is why I was so sad to hear what happened to him.'

'Do you believe all that stuff about him killing General Balmes?'

'Well, it's what I heard my father tell my mother, all those years ago, and it's also what Pedro—*Father* Pedro—says in his account, and I certainly have no reason to question it.'

'Yes, I wanted to ask you about that...' Velázquez leaned forward, elbows on knees. 'You say in your manuscript that Father Pedro's account was actually written by him... is that true?'

'Oh yes, absolutely.'

'Why would he have sent you an account of what he'd been up to like that, do you think?'

'Well, I really have no idea, Inspector.' Anna Segura shrugged. 'You'd have to ask him that.'

'As you know, I'm not in a position to do that, so I was wondering if I could perhaps pick your brain?'

She shrugged. 'I suppose he sent it to me because he was in love with me when he was young.'

'So it was for old times' sake, then, you think?'

'Something like that, I suppose…'

Anna Segura got up and took her handbag from the marble-topped coffee table, then rummaged around in it until she found her Marlboros, along with a lighter. There was a nervous, jerky quality to her movements; she was a ball of energy, and her limbs were all stringy and sinewy, quite free of fat. She dropped the handbag, a little Dolce and Gabbana number, onto the table, then sat down again before she took a cigarette from the pack and lit up. 'Was there anything else, Inspector Jefe?' She took a long drag on her Marlboro, and squinted at Velázquez through a shifting cloud of silky smoke.

Velázquez glanced at his watch; he'd better hurry up and finish the interview if he was going to make it out to the bullring in time to see the *corrida*. Pe would kill him if he didn't.

'There is one more thing, Señora Segura,' he said. 'I was just wondering if you edited the account that Father Pedro sent you, or if his account appears verbatim and in its entirety in your manuscript?'

'No, I kept it just as it was.' She took another long drag on her Marlboro. 'Didn't cut or change a single word.'

Velázquez and Gajardo hurried back to the Iglesia de Jesús del Gran Poder. The Inspector Jefe parked up a side street, then he and Gajardo entered the church and found Father Antonio. 'I'm afraid there's been some more bad news,' Velázquez said.

'What's happened?'

'Perhaps you should sit down…'

'Just tell me, will you?'

'I'm afraid Father Aloysius has been murdered.'

The priest appeared to wobble, and looked for a moment as though he might be about to fall, so that Velázquez reached out a hand to steady him. 'I'm very sorry, Father.'

Velázquez gave the priest a moment to compose himself; then Father Antonio said, 'But how did it happen?'

'He was found in the river… otherwise, it was the same

modus operandi as was used on Father Pedro, which means it's almost certainly the same killer.'

'Have you any idea who did it?'

'Not as yet, which is why I was wondering if you might be able to help me?'

'Help you…?'

'Did Father Aloysius have any enemies that you know of?'

'I wouldn't know about that, but I do know that he had a tendency to express ideas and views that many people found controversial, to say the least… it was something he had in common with Father Pedro.'

'They were good friends, I believe…?'

'Yes… and they both held the view that the Vatican had some explaining to do over its recent past.'

'In supporting the Franco regime, you mean?'

'Exactly… they were liberals, modernizers, if you will… and they both felt that the Catholic Church has made something of a habit of failing to stand up for the interests of the people when the chips are down.'

Gajardo said, 'And what do you think about that, Father Antonio?'

'I suppose they had a point.'

'Must be difficult being a priest when you hold ideas like that, I should've thought?'

'Being a priest is never easy, and nor was it meant to be.'

'Why go to all the trouble, then?' Velázquez asked.

'I can best answer that question with a single word, Inspector Jefe: faith.'

'But you sound as though you agree with Fathers Pedro and Aloysius that the Church was batting on the wrong side back in the Civil War.'

'I believe, as they did, I think, that the Church should stand up for the weak and the downtrodden.'

'And the meek shall inherit the earth, is that it, Father?'

'Exactly… only back then the Church was in a difficult

position... After all, it could hardly have aligned itself with Stalin's Russia, when Stalin was murdering millions of his own people, could it? And besides, Stalin had banned organized religion.'

'Why couldn't it have resisted both the fascists and the communists and stood up for the path of freedom and liberal democracy?'

'It was felt at the time that liberal democracy had no future in Spain—or indeed in Europe... Remember the Civil War was, in the eyes of many, a dry run for the Second World War; and since the British and the Americans refused to get involved, it was generally believed that we in Spain were faced with a stark choice—it was either one thing or the other.'

'All seems rather black and white, don't you think?' Gajardo said.

'If you'd heard the sermons Fathers Pedro and Aloysius gave, you'd know that is what they felt—*Manichean* was the word they used for it... What can I say, Inspector?' The priest shrugged. 'You are a Spaniard, so you hardly need me to tell you what we are like; we are a people who tend to go to extremes... It seems as though somebody who didn't appreciate what they had to say was just as willing to go to extremes as they were... '

'You mean you think they could have been murdered because of their political views?'

'It's the only reason I can think of.'

Velázquez said, 'Can you give us any names, Father?'

'*Names*, Inspector Jefe...?'

'Of parishioners who might have born a grudge against the two priests?'

'No, I'm sorry but nobody springs to mind.'

'I think I should warn you, Father Antonio, that you need to be on your guard from now on.'

'But what makes you say that, Inspector Jefe?'

'Think about it, Father... the other two priests who served at this church have both been murdered in the same manner.'

Father Antonio's eyes flashed and his purplish lips parted as the penny finally appeared to drop. 'You don't mean to say that—'

'It's a possibility that the killer could come after you next, yes.'

'But my sermons have never been anywhere near as controversial as those of Fathers Pedro and Aloysius, Inspector Jefe.'

'I thought you just said you agreed with their views?'

'I do, yes, but even so…'

Velázquez narrowed his eyes, like he was confused about something. 'I don't quite follow you.'

Father Antonio shrugged. 'I shared their take on what happened in the past, but I disagreed with their decision to talk about their views so openly.'

'And why do you think they did that?'

'They felt, as many people do, that we Spaniards will never be able to escape from our past and move on until we face up to the truth of what happened, and are able to talk about it openly.'

'And you disagree?'

'I think it's sometimes better to let sleeping dogs lie.'

Velázquez took a chew on his fleshy lower lip. 'If the killer or killers singled Fathers Pedro and Aloysius out for revenge as a result of what they talked about in their sermons, then it's likely that you have nothing to worry about, Father… But I must warn you that I can't be at all sure of that right now. Nothing is certain.'

'So what are you saying exactly?'

'Use your common sense, and don't take any chances… If someone calls asking you to go to their home, just say you're too busy… Avoid walking in dark, isolated places on your own at night—car parks, that kind of thing.' Velázquez turned to go; then he stopped and reached into his pocket and brought out his card. 'And please call me if anything occurs to you, or if anything unusual happens, okay?—and I mean *anything*.'

63

CHAPTER 8

'… and that concludes the review of yesterday's bullfights at Las Ventas —'; Velázquez turned the radio off. Moments later, he pulled up outside his flat, hurried inside and shot up in the kitchen. Then he drove back to Forensics, to pick up Gómez, and they headed off for the bullring.

They hadn't gone far before he began to worry about Pe and the coming *corrida*, and his nerves were in tatters by the time they finally got there. Worse still, it occurred to Velázquez that if Pe were to realize her dream of becoming a professional bullfighter then he would have to go through this on a *regular basis*.

It wouldn't have been so bad if he didn't love her so much.

He figured he was just going to have to put his foot down and tell Pe the way he felt.

Only he'd already tried that… and it hadn't worked.

Velazquez and Gomez found a couple of seats near the *barrera*, where they would have a perfect view of everything. Gómez produced a small flask from his breast pocket and took a swig, before offering it to Velázquez. 'It's Scotch… might help to calm your nerves a little.'

'Why–do I look like I'm nervous?'

Gómez grinned. 'Is the Pope a Catholic?'

Velázquez took a swig of the Scotch; it ran down his throat like fire.

First *tercio*, first *matador* up: young lad of twenty or so strolled into the ring along with his team of *peones*. Capes windmilled round the bull, teasing, warming him up, then the *picadors* started in.

Velázquez's thoughts returned to the case during the rest of the first and second *tercios*, and he only really began to focus on what was happening in the ring once more during the final *suerte*, when the young bullfighter went in for the kill. The *matador* stood stock still. The music started. He lined up his sword. Velazquez thought the lad was rather tall for a bullfighter and cut an ungainly figure. The music stopped. The bullfighter cried '*Toro!*' and again '*Toro!*' —and the beast charged.

The lad ran to meet it, thrust his sword into the animal's neck, and jumped aside in a jerky, uneven movement. The sword went flying through the air and landed some distance away. The lad scampered after it, and only regained his cool when he had the sword back in his hand.

Now Velázquez saw Pe appear in the *callejon* and go behind the *burlador* to follow the action in the arena. The bullfighter lined up his sword once more and cried: '*Toro!*' and again: '*Toro!*' and the tired animal charged. This time, the bullfighter managed to get the sword to stay in the animal's neck, but the beast refused to go down.

It took him six attempts to kill the bull, and the overall impression was, needless to say, rather less than satisfactory. The crowd was getting restless by the end, and there were some jeers.

Next it was the turn of Pe and her team, and Velázquez's belly turned over as he watched her stroll out into the ring. She looked as though she were completely alone with her own thoughts. Velázquez crossed himself and said a quick prayer. Gómez saw him and followed suit.

The first *tercio* began. The bull charged one of the horses from the side, hooking up repeatedly with its horns. The horse was wearing armour, and the *picador* jabbed at the bull with his lance and drew blood. Then the *banderillero* made his entrance and the bull switched its attention to him. The *banderillo* waited until the last moment, before neatly stepping aside and stabbing the animal in the neck with his *banderillas*, to the applause of the crowd. Having done what was expected of him, the *bandillero* sped off and skipped behind the *burlador*.

Pe strutted over to the bull and drew it towards the centre

of the ring, then stood, taut and still, her cape stretched out in front of her. The bull stood before her and stamped its hoof; it charged, hooking upward with its horns as it filled the cape and passed through it, its energy now turning to anger at missing its target.

Next Pe made to execute another *media veronica*, but midway through she went over the bull's horn and turned her back on the animal as it followed the cape. This brought applause and cries of '*Olé*' from the crowd and the band struck up a *pasodoble*, in tribute to Pe's *faena*.

Pe carried on like that. Her movements were as easy and supple as a cat's: hypnotic, rhythmic and, like all the most difficult and beautiful things in this world, apparently effortless. Velázquez marvelled at her skill in silence while the crowd roared out another chorus of '*olé's*', making the air tremble with its applause. The band started up once more. Gómez touched Velázquez on the arm and said, 'This is *real* bullfighting.'

Velázquez turned fear-wracked eyes on his friend; his only immediate concern was that Pe shouldn't get hurt. The quality of her work was the last thing on his mind.

'No, I really mean it,' Gómez said, mistaking the fear and anxiety in Velázquez's expression for disbelief. 'She's far too good to be appearing in a small ring like this.'

Velázquez turned back to watch Pe perform another *veronica*, followed by a *larga cordobesa*, a pass which ended with the cape resting on her shoulder. Another fanfare from the band; another chorus of '*olés*' and applause from the crowd. It was clear to Velázquez that the crowd had really warmed to Pe. She had washed away the bad feeling left by the rather inept young *matador* earlier.

The music stopped, only for it to begin again moments later to announce the beginning of the final *suerte*. The crowd quietened down; Pe lined up her sword and sighted the bull along it. This was the last and most important part of the bullfight. Even though Pe had performed brilliantly up until now, every pass that she made having been executed with unhurried mastery, it might all count for nothing if she failed to make an effective kill. The vital area in the animal's neck was no bigger than a *cien-peseta* coin. If you missed the small target but still got the sword in the bull's neck then you might strike bone, and, like the previous *matador*, suffer the indignity of seeing your sword go swirling through the air.

The bull charged. Pe waited. It got closer and closer… and then, just as it seemed she had left it too late and there was no escaping the bull's horns, she jumped to the side and rammed her sword into just the right place… The bull collapsed head-first into the sand, blood pouring from its mouth. The small crowd went wild as the band started to play…

Velázquez dropped Gómez off at his place in Triana before crossing the river and heading for home; and no sooner had he and Pe entered the flat than his mobile began to ring. '*Hola*?'

'Traced your old car, Boss—the Alfa Romeo.'

'Good man. Where was it?'

'Somebody used it in a hit and run attack.'

'They *what*…?'

'The *Científicos* are still going over it at the moment, see if they can come up with any DNA or prints,' Gajardo said. 'Told me they'll return it to the impound when they've finished with it, so you should be able to pick it up from there in the morning… And you'll never guess who the victim is—only our friend Ramón Ochoa.'

'*Joder*… Is he okay?'

'He's in the Hospital de la Macarena… last I heard he was still in a coma.'

'*Cojones*… Have you been in to see him?'

'Not yet.'

Pe announced that she was going to take a shower, and

Velázquez told her he needed to go out. 'Won't be too late, will you?'

'Shouldn't be,' he said and blew her a kiss as he left the flat. He drove down Calle Teodosio, turned off, and zigzagged through the streets until he reached Calle Feria, then drove along it right to the end, past the fish market and bars and shops on either side. Turned right into busy Calle Resolana, went past the Macarena Basilica and the *puerta de la Macarena*, one of the gateways through which the walled city could be entered when it was built back in the twelfth century, then swept up past the Parlamento de Andalucía, and the Macarena Hospital was just over on the left. He pulled into the parking area outside to see a posse of journalists and cameramen standing over by the front steps, waiting for him. Velázquez cursed, shitting in the milk under his breath, as he hurried over towards the steps. One of the pack spotted him, and the next moment he found himself moving slowly through a gauntlet of reporters all barking questions at him: how was the victim? And how was it that Ramón Ochoa had ended up in hospital in the first place? Velázquez kept saying 'No comment', trying to look impassive. The pack stuck with him all the way up the steps, but he managed to squeeze in through the glass doors, then hurried over to the peroxide blonde on reception, and told her that he'd come to see Ramón Ochoa.

The woman picked up the phone and after a brief exchange told him *señor* Ochoa was in no state to receive visitors. In that case, perhaps he could speak to the doctor who was treating him?

He had to wait for the doctor to come down. To cut a story short, Ochoa was still in a coma, and the doctor could not say what his chances of recovery were.

Velazquez left his number and drove home.

No sooner had the Inspector Jefe climbed out of the car than he was hit by a wave of giddiness and nausea. He needed a fix and knew he'd only get worse until he had one. Problem was, he had no heroin left. I need to go and score, he thought, or I'm fucked.

Best place to score horse was either over on the Alameda de Hercules, or out in the Tres Mil Viviendas. The Tres Mil was the best bet, he figured: far less chance of being spotted by one of his colleagues.

He was about to get back in the Seat Ibiza when he thought better of it: more sensible to get a taxi, because you couldn't park anywhere in that part of town without running a serious risk of having your car stolen. So he walked the short distance over to the Plaza del Duque, climbed into the back of the first taxi in the rank, and told the driver where he wanted to go.

'I don't go to the Tres Mil,' the driver said. 'You won't get anybody else to take you there, either. Too dangerous... especially at this time of night.'

'Okay, well take me as close to it as you can, then.'

They set off, and after they'd gone some way the driver said, 'You live there?'

'No.'

'Didn't think so.' The driver was looking at Velázquez in his mirror. 'Don't seem like the kind of person who'd be living in a place like that, if I might say so... Sure you still want to go there?'

'Yes.'

'It's just that the place has got a terrible reputation, you know,' the man said. 'Some of the stories I've heard are enough to put me off going there, I know that much.'

'What stories are these, then?'

'They've stopped taxis and made the drivers get out at gunpoint, taken everything from them, including the car... drivers have had to walk back... one came back in his underwear.'

'What about the police, don't they do anything?'

'People reckon the cops are too frightened to go in there as well, unless they go in large numbers and armed to the teeth,' the cabby said. 'But what's a smartly dressed gent like you want to be going to the Tres Mil for, if you don't mind my asking?'

'I'm a police detective.'

'Oh, I see. That explains it.'

No it doesn't, Velázquez thought. Not by a long chalk.

'After a criminal down there, are you?'

'That's right.'

'Where's your police car, then?'

'Hardly want to announce the fact I'm a policeman.'

'Oh, I get it… undercover, are you?'

'That's it.'

Velázquez was getting tired of the man's questions; he took to replying in monosyllables until the cabby got the message and they headed on through the suburbs in silence. Then when they got to the other side of Bami, the cabby pulled over. 'This is as far as I go.'

Velázquez paid the fare, got out and started walking.

It was dark and there weren't many people about. He passed a bar full of old guys sitting talking over a drink, and pressed on until he eventually found himself at the start of a street lined with warehouses. In architectural terms, this area was the polar opposite of the Old Quarter. In simple terms, the place was a dump. Not only that, but it was a *dangerous* dump, especially if you were an outsider. A little posse of prostitutes were standing on the corner. They were dressed for the beach or bedroom, in bikinis or else a tanga with stockings and high heels. One was topless. They called to Velázquez as he passed. 'How about taking a trip to Mars, *hombre*?'

'Thought that's where I was,' Velázquez felt like telling them, but didn't.

Turning the next corner, he found himself on a long, broad street. A rubbish container had been tipped over, its contents left sprawling over the pavement, and the pavements themselves were a jigsaw of broken stones and grass. A wild dog went running past, and then Velázquez came to a bar. There were a number of motorbikes parked outside.

Velázquez entered the place, and was immediately struck by the smell of disinfectant and marijuana. Or *maría*, as the locals called it. The men at the counter turned and stared at Velázquez. They were all dressed in leathers and some of them had shaved heads. Biker types. Velázquez acted like he didn't notice all the attention he was getting. The barman came over and made a show of looking him up and down. The man was an enormous chunk of formless cement with a couple of kegs of beer hidden under his black T-shirt and a forest of greasy black beard. 'You new here,' he said. It wasn't a question.

Velázquez said, 'The matter, you only serve regulars?'

'Depends what people come here lookin' for.'

'I need to score a wrap of horse.'

The man looked at him in stony silence for a moment, as did the bikers. Velázquez could hear the whir of a propeller fan. 'Wouldn't be a *poli*, would you?'

'Do I *look* like one?'

The man shrugged. 'Look like shit, so you could be.'

'*Polis* usually come in here saying they need to score heroin?'

'Even *polis* ain't usually *that* stupid.'

CHAPTER 9

'Well,' Velázquez said, 'either you can help me or you can't... You know anyone who's selling around here?'

One of the bikers took a last drag on his joint, then gestured to Velázquez, got off his stool and headed for the toilet. He was your typical biker, down to the greasy ponytail and swastika on the jacket lapel. But Velázquez followed him anyway, and no sooner had the toilet door slammed shut behind him than the Inspector Jefe was shoved back against the wall. It was too dark to see anything, and he felt a cold metal blade against his throat. The biker must have flicked the switch by the door, because the light came on. 'The fuck is this?' Velázquez said.

'Think they call it a knife.' The man's long thin lips parted in a reptile grin. 'Blade's nice 'n sharp... What do you want here?'

'I need to score some heroin, like I said... What's with the knife, *hombre*...?'

'You better not be a cop.'

'I told you, I need a fix.'

'I heard you... only you look like a cop to me.'

'Just sell me some horse and I'll be on my way.'

The man lowered the knife and took a step backwards. 'I dunno about you, *hombre*... you got something about you... certain look I don't trust.'

'For fuck's sake, I need a fix I tell you... Look at my forehead. I'm clammy with sweat. I need to score. *Cojones!*'

'How much you want?'

'How much for four wraps?'

'Thirty thousand *pesetas*.'

'That's way too steep.'

The man shrugged.

Velázquez figured he didn't have much choice. 'Okay.'

The man continued to look at him, like he was trying to make up his mind. Then he said, 'Okay, wait here,' and went out.

Minutes later, he returned and said, 'Looks like it's your lucky day.' The man reached into his pocket and pulled out a little baggie. 'Didn't come in wraps this time,' he said. 'Have to take it like this.'

Velázquez felt he was being tricked. 'That's less than four wraps.'

'Looks like more to me.' The man shrugged. 'Price is thirty thousand *pesetas*. Take it or leave it.'

Velázquez reached into his pocket and took out the money. The man snatched the banknotes and pocketed them before he handed over the baggie. 'Wait in here a coupla minutes before you come out.'

'Okay... but what's the big deal? Don't get cops down this way, do you?'

'Normally when they come here, they come in numbers and armed to the teeth. But you never know, might get a lone *poli* sent here undercover, to spy on us.'

The man leered at Velázquez again, then he turned and went out. Velázquez waited for a couple of minutes, like the man said, before he came out of the bathroom. He was sweating by now and feeling like he had a fever. His legs were weak, everything seemed distant, as if in a film.

Once out of the bar, he glanced over his shoulder to check he wasn't being followed. He went back the way he'd come, going back past the bar he'd seen earlier. There were still a few old boys sitting in there, chatting over a drink. Men with nobody to go home to. Velázquez hurried on. He had to get home, fast.

2

TERCIO DE BANDERILLAS.

The matador *waited for the bull until the last fraction of a second. It seemed as though the horn was about to go in, that the* matador *had left it too late; but then he rammed the sticks in and skipped clear all in one supple movement.*

CHAPTER 10

Velázquez checked that Pe was asleep in bed as soon as he got back to the flat; and minutes later, he was wandering through his favourite playground in Seventh Heaven once more.

He went into the living room and turned the television on, slap bang in the middle of a report on the murder case: *'As yet no arrests have been made. Sources close to the police force have revealed that Homicide detectives are running around chasing their own tails. In addition, an Alfa Romeo was found abandoned after a hit and run incident in which a young Sevillano, Ramón Ochoa, was knocked down.*

'Senor Ochoa is now in hospital, where we understand that he is in a coma. It seems that the car, which has been traced to Inspector Jefe Velázquez del Grupo de Homicidios, was used in an attempt on the young man's life...'

Then Velázquez saw himself on the screen walking up the steps at the front of the Macarena hospital, surrounded by reporters. Saw himself there, looking furious but trying not to let it show as he kept saying 'No comment' in response to the reporters' questions... Just fucking great, he thought, and cursed under his breath, shitting in the milk as his own angry mug filled the screen. Looked like a bull cornered by a *matador* and his *picador* and *banderilleros* for a moment... and then, mercifully, his face was gone and the anchor moved onto the next news item.

Velázquez figured the little report he'd just watched was probably the PR nightmare to end all PR nightmares; but he would be buggered sideways by a bull if he was going to let it get to him. Bad enough as it was, without his joining in on the side of his oppressors. Spain for you, he thought. Kind of people we are. Nation of folk who're always on the lookout for a bull to stick a *pica* or sword into. Right now, he was the *toro*. Thankfully, he was much too high to let it really get to him. *Screw the bastards.*

Wasn't long before he began to feel kind of antsy, though, and going to sleep was the last thing he wanted to do; so he went over to the *Jefatura* to pick up Anna Seguro's manuscript, brought it home with him, then stretched out on the sofa and began to read, picking up where he'd left off…

One of my fellow prisoners, a German lad called Klaus, said he wanted out of the war. He planned to escape and asked if I wanted to go with him. But I was convinced that our forces would break through any day, and I longed for them to come and rescue us. Or at least, I did at first—until Klaus, who had been flying with the Condor Legion of the German Luftwaffe that destroyed Guernica, told me how the bombing was authorized by German feldmarschall Wolfram Von Richthofen, and ultimately therefore also by General Franco himself. When I heard that I lost all faith in the Nationalist cause and decided to escape; so when the reinforcements stormed the makeshift camp the following day, I seized my opportunity…

Pedro went on to describe how he came across an injured Anarchist whom he helped back to his people in the mountains. Once there, Pedro was able to pass himself off as a fellow Republican, and worked hard to try to escape his past…

And he very nearly succeeded in doing so, Velázquez thought.

But not quite, of course…

Velázquez yawned and glanced at his Swatch. It was coming up to three-thirty a.m. and his eyelids felt loaded with lead weights. He put the manuscript down, then lay back on the sofa and shut his eyes, and the next moment he was fast asleep. Only sleep, when it came nowadays, rarely offered him any respite from the thoughts that troubled him during his waking hours, and it was no different on this occasion. He was sitting in a chair, blindfolded, and the Black Lady was giving him a load of flannel about New Orleans that he didn't believe a word of: he'd be surprised if she'd been further afield than Dos Hermanas, and he told her as much. 'Now, now,' Bill said, 'you ought to know better than to treat the Black Lady like that... specially seeing as she's come all this way just for you.'

Then the needle went in.

And he woke up.

Feeling clammy and sick, he stumbled out to the bathroom and splashed cold water over his face. Stood looking at himself in the mirror, taking in the unhealthy-looking skin, the wild eyes with their broken veins...

Found himself wondering whether they were the eyes of a man who was in his right mind.

Velázquez drove over to the impound to pick up his old Alfa Romeo first thing the following morning, happy to get it back and not at all sad to see the back of the Seat Ibiza. Then he drove to the *Jefatura* and worked on his report for an hour.

He'd just taken a sip of the liquefied mud Serrano had brought him, courtesy of the machine downstairs, when the telephone on his desk began to ring. '*Diga?*'

'This is Doctor Sanchez.'

'*Hola,* Doctor... What's happened? Has there been a change in Ramón Ochoa's condition?'

'Yes, I'm very happy to say that he has rejoined us in the land of the living.'

'That's great news. Can I come over and talk to him now?'

'So long as you keep it short and sweet, Inspector Jefe... I'm sure I don't need to remind you that he's still in the recovery stage.'

'Of course.'

Velázquez rose from his chair and Gajardo looked over. 'Off somewhere, Boss?'

'Ochoa's come out of the coma.'

'That case, I'll come with you.'

79

'No, I'll handle this alone. You'd be better employed knocking on more doors round where Father Aloysius lived. Take Merino with you.'

'What about me, Boss?' Agente Pérez asked. 'Want me to go with them?'

'Yes, but first you can get onto Ballistics for me, Sara, and see if they can tell us anything yet about the two bullets that were found in the vics.'

'Right you are… and I'll call you if they've come up with something, yeah?'

'Straightaway.'

Agente Serrano said, 'Got something particular in mind you want me to do, Boss?'

'Go over to Jesus del Gran Poder, Jorge, and talk to whoever you can.'

Velázquez had taken his jacket from the back of his chair and was now working his arms into it. 'Try to find out if either of the murdered priests have any siblings, close friends or relations who are still alive. If so then find out where they live and go and talk to them, if they are living in or around Seville.'

Serrano took the lift down with Velázquez.

'It's highly likely that siblings and relatives aren't going to take very kindly to your asking about the victims' sexuality, Jorge, so you're going to have to show a little tact.'

'I'll impress on them how relevant it is to the investigation, Boss.'

Ramón Ochoa was sitting up in bed when Velázquez entered the room at the hospital. The lad was hooked up to a spider's web of tubes, and one of his hands was chained to the iron bedframe; he looked pale and a little dazed, but he was conscious. Velázquez smiled and said, 'Glad to see you're back with us, Ramón… we were all worried about you for a while back there.'

Ochoa looked terrified and called for the guard. Seeing his reaction, Velázquez held up his hands and said, 'I haven't come here to do you any harm.'

'It was your car that hit me.'

'I know... whoever hit you stole it.'

'How can I know you aren't lying?'

'Why'd I want to kill you?'

'I've no idea.'

'No, and that's because I have no reason to... But there's somebody out there who wants you silenced for good... and whoever it is reckoned it would be a good idea to kill you and frame me for your murder.'

'Why'd they wanna do that?'

'That's easy... they wanted me off the case.'

Ramón Ochoa said, 'Only thing I know for sure's that the driver intended to hit me.'

'See who was driving?'

Ochoa shook his head. 'All happened too quickly.'

'How did you know it was my car, then?'

'Mum told me... she saw it on the News.'

'I'm here to help, Ramón... but I need you to tell me what you know if we're going to catch this guy.'

'Help put me away, you mean?'

'Not necessarily.'

Ramón moved his right hand and jangled the chain against the iron bed-frame. 'I'm supposed to've killed a couple of priests, hadn't you heard?'

'I don't necessarily buy into that.'

The sneer that had been on Ramón Ochoa's face disappeared, and he looked like he was interested in what Velázquez might have to say. 'What does *necessarily* mean exac'ly...?'

'What you think it means,' Velázquez said. 'I want to hear what you've got to say...'

'I don't get it.' Ochoa pulled a face. 'I'm framed for the murder of Father Pedro, then Father Aloysius is killed, and it looks like I'm the prime suspect for both of them, but it's all bullshit... Why'd I wanna go bumping off a couple of priests?'

Doctor Sanchez entered the room at that moment. 'Inspector Jefe, I'm afraid your time's up,' he said. 'I really must insist that you leave the patient to get some rest now.'

'Okay—thanks for answering my questions, Ramón.' Velázquez left the room with Doctor Sanchez.

'He going to be okay now, Doc?'

'I should think so.' Doctor Sanchez pushed the button to call the lift. 'But I really must stress how important it is that he should be allowed to rest.'

'Of course. Thanks for keeping me informed and letting me see him.'

'Anything I can do to help a fellow professional, Inspector Jefe—just so long as it doesn't harm the patient.'

The doors of the lift opened. Velázquez stepped in, pushed the button for the ground floor, and stared at the numbers above the doors lighting up in red as he descended. He was starting to feel clammy again, and realized that it wouldn't be long before he needed his next fix.

CHAPTER 11

Velázquez passed through the glass doors, ran down the steps, and was heading across the car park when a navy-blue BMW came speeding towards him. He held up an arm, but instead of slowing down, the car speeded up. Velázquez began to run. The car came straight at him. He dived through the air and landed on the bonnet of a parked Mercedes just as the BMW went hurtling past, its wheels screeching as it turned at the end of the gangway. The windows of the vehicle were tinted, so there was no way of seeing the driver; but he did manage to get a look at the reg as the vehicle passed out of the car park and joined the main road.

A man ran over as Velázquez got down off the bonnet of the Mercedes. 'I saw that,' the man said. 'The son of the great whore drove straight at you like he tried to hit you.'

'He *did* try to hit me.'

'Are you okay?'

Velázquez nodded, then took out notepad and pen, and made a note of the reg on the BMW.

'That was quite a dive you made there... sure you haven't hurt yourself?'

'No, I'm fine... but thanks for your concern.'

'D'you want me to call the police for you, or help you into the hospital?'

'No.' Velázquez smiled. 'It's okay. I'm a policeman.'

'Oh... well, if you're sure you don't need any help...' The man went on his way, and Velázquez continued to his car, got in and set off out of the car park. He passed the Parlamento de Andalucía and the Macarena church, where the bullfighters were supposed to pray before a *corrida*, then went up busy Calle Feria.

He pulled over outside a Basque bar. Men were standing outside on the pavement, talking, one or two of them wearing traditional Basque berets. Velázquez hopped out onto the cobbles, locked the doors, and headed off to his left. He crossed a square, passed a small supermarket, walked up a narrow street, then took a right, and the clinic was at the end on the corner. It was a modern building, with white walls and lots of glass so that you could see inside. He went in and made an emergency appointment.

The man behind the counter gave him a slip of paper. Velázquez looked at the two numbers: the doctor's room number, and his own number in the queue. He went and found the room. Four other people were sitting in plastic chairs by the door. He sat down to wait.

And while he waited, he began to feel more and more like he needed a fix.

He wondered who had been driving the blue BMW.

Still wondering, he took out his mobile and called Gajardo.

'*Hola*, Boss… you okay?'

'Yeah, but only because I got lucky.'

'What happened?'

'Blue BMW drove at me in the car park outside the Hospital de la Macarena,' Velázquez said. 'Only just managed to jump out of the way in time.'

'See who was driving?'

'No, the windows were tinted… but I've got the reg. I need you to run a check for me.'

'Sure. Fire away.'

Velázquez opened his notepad and read out the registration number.

'I'll check it out now, Boss, and get back to you as soon as I've got something,' Gajardo said. 'Where are you?'

'I'm at the doctor's, just to get myself checked out.'

'I was about to call you, actually.'

'What's happened?'

'Judge Montero made a call to your desk a short while ago, and I took it for you… He wants to know if we've got a case or not.'

'Tell him we're working on it.'

'Already did, but he didn't sound too impressed. Said we've got twenty-four hours to come up with something, otherwise it's no go.'

'Better get cracking, then.'

'Too right, Boss… Anyway, I'll check out that reg for you.'

They hung up, and Velázquez's thoughts turned on the sections of Anna Segura's manuscript that he'd read. Had the young Pedro Mora really assassinated General Balmes? he wondered. And if so, then was it possible that the priest might have been killed by a member of Balmes's family out to take revenge?

Two arguments against this possible line of enquiry immediately occurred to Velázquez. First, only four people would have known that it was Pedro Mora who killed Balmes (presuming Anna Segura's account could be trusted), and those were Pedro Mora himself, and Anna Segura and her parents.

Second, if a member of Balmes's family really had killed Father Mora to take revenge, then why would they have waited all this time in order to take action?

It was always possible that the killer only found out that it was Father Mora fairly recently, though, Velázquez thought.

It occurred to him that if somebody in Balmes's family had discovered the identity of the General's assassin, then it must mean that either: A) more than four people had known about it, in which case Anna Segura's account could not be trusted totally; or: B) one of the four who were party to the secret—that is, either Anna Segura or one of her parents, or Father Pedro Mora himself—must have divulged the identity of the assassin to a third party, and that struck Velázquez as being highly unlikely.

The lady in the grey trouser-suit who had been before Velázquez in the queue came out through the door. The Inspector Jefe stood up and went in. The doctor, fair-haired and bespectacled, smiled and asked Velázquez what she could do for him. 'I need a week's supply of methadone.' Velázquez found his wallet, took out his health card and handed it to the doctor.

Then his mobile began to ring. '*Diga?*'

'Velázquez, Comisario Alonso here. There's been another murder...'

CHAPTER 12

The victim was lying naked on the bed, and he had been shot in the head. A fingerprint expert, wearing custom-made inspection glasses, was sticking pieces of tape to the bed frame, wall and bedside table. Wherever he saw a print, he'd peel the tape off and store it.

No sign of a knife on this one, and the victim had been shot in the head, which could well mean this was the work of a different killer. The bullet had gone in above the ear, so that much of the skull was destroyed, with blood and bits of flesh and bone splashed over the walls. Despite this, the victim's face was relatively untouched. Foreign, thought Velázquez. Possibly Russian.

Judge Cristobal Montero entered the room, followed by Subinspector Gajardo, both in immaculate suits, unlike Velázquez. Once again he reminded himself he wasn't in some Hollywood flick.

'*Hola*, Boss, Judge Montero,' Gajardo said. 'Got here as soon as I could.' He seemed to be out of breath as he looked at the victim lying on the bed.

Judge Montero shook his head and said, 'What a bloody mess.'

'Looks like he was taken by surprise,' Subinspector Gajardo observed. 'Could even have been asleep when he was shot, by the look of him.'

'What I was just thinking,' Velázquez concurred.

'However it happened,' the Judge said, 'we can't have people killing each other right left and centre like this, Inspector Jefe.'

Gajardo said, '*Científicos* on their way, Boss?'

Velázquez nodded as the door opened, and Juan Gómez entered the room. 'Good afternoon, gentlemen,' he said, as he came over to the bed and put his briefcase down.

'Wouldn't go that far,' Velázquez said.

The Inspector Jefe drove to the Poligono Sur, pulled over and parked in one jerky manouvre, then climbed out of the car. His trousers and the back of his shirt were sticking to his skin as he made his way towards the entrance to the club. The word BLONDES was written up in big bold letters outside, reflecting no doubt its ungentlemanly owner's general preference where the fair sex was concerned. Odd choice for a name, you might think, in a city where blondes were generally thought to be thin on the ground… except they weren't, of course, because they came all the way from Eastern Europe to work in dumps like this one.

Diego Blanco, the club's proprietor, was known to the police, and to Velázquez in particular. Truth to tell, the Inspector Jefe had spent a good part of the previous ten years trying to nail the gangster on a whole litany of charges; but somehow he'd always failed to do so. You could say the two men had become the best of enemies, and it was certainly true that Velázquez hated the man's guts. The fact remained, though, that little happened in the city's criminal underworld without Blanco knowing about it, which was why Velázquez had chosen to come and pay a call on the man now.

It was dark in the club and the place seemed to be doing a fairly good trade, despite the fact that it had only just turned noon. Velázquez spotted Diego Blanco sitting on a stool over at the bar, holding court to a bevy of young women. All of the girls had big breasts, which they seemed to be trying to thrust into the gangster's face. Like some competition, Velázquez thought, where the girl who gets to show the most cleavage wins; and, needless to say, there was a wealth of Botox and silicone on show. Not that Diego Blanco seemed to mind. The guy was clearly in his element. Look at him, with his gut pressing against his Lacoste polo shirt, *torero*'s ponytail, leather waistcoat unbuttoned, Cuban cigar poking between stubby fingers studded with gold rings so thick they'd serve as knuckledusters. Man looked as though he'd gone to a lot of trouble and expense in order to look that tacky.

Velázquez went up to the bar and asked for a large Johnnie, neat. 'Black or red?'

'Black,' Diego Blanco called through the melee. 'And it's on me.'

Velázquez turned and said, 'See you've got company.'

The gangster shrugged as if to say *What can you do...?* Then said, 'To what do I owe the pleasure?'

'Just thought I'd call in for a chat.'

'Always were one to like a chinwag, Inspector Jefe.'

The barman put Velázquez's drink down on the counter. 'There somewhere we can talk without all this'—he waved his hand—'...interference?'

'Sure.' Diego Blanco clicked his fingers and the sea of cleavages parted. The next moment, the two men were sitting alone at the bar.

Velázquez said, 'Been a spate of murders in the city of late, Diego, case you hadn't noticed.'

'Ask me, this city's gettin' worse than fuckin' *Chee*-ca-go. *Joder!*'

Velázquez nodded, sipped his Scotch. 'Don't suppose you'd know anything about any of it?'

'Any of what...?'

'All these murders...?'

'No, nothing to do with me, Inspector Jefe.'

'Wasn't my question.'

'*Que...?*'

'Didn't say it was anything to do with you, Diego.'

'Glad to hear it.'

'Only I think it's fair to say you normally have a good idea of what's going down in this city.'

'Have my fingers in a number of pies, it's true,' the gangster said. 'But I don't know nothin' about any of these murders, I can tell you that much.'

'Nice Scotch,' Velázquez said.

'Have another.' Diego Blanco gestured to the barman, then pointed to the Inspector Jefe's glass. The barman poured Velázquez another large one, set it down on the counter in front of him.

'Nice club you've got here, Diego,' Velázquez said. 'Be a shame if I had to call the attention of certain of my colleagues to one or two of the less legal things that tend to happen on the premises from time to time.'

'No need to get like that, is there?' Blanco objected. 'You come in waltzing in here and I make you welcome, give you a coupla Johnnie Blacks on the house and now you're givin' me this shit. You gotta be taking me by the hair, right?'

'I asked you a question, Diego, and I never got an answer.'

'Look,' the gangster said, 'it's the fuckin' Russkies, ain't it.'

'What is…?'

'Fuckin' city's been going downhill ever since they set up shop here earlier in the year… fuckin' bad news, they are.'

'Sound a little xenophobic, Diego.'

'Ain't that, exactly… I mean, I ain't got nothin' against our Russian friends, it's just that I don't want the bastards over 'ere, tha's all. I mean what's the matter with fuckin' Russia? Ain't the place big enough for 'em?'

'So it's all down to the Russians, you're telling me.'

'*Sí.*'

'That's easy to say,' Velázquez said. 'But it doesn't tell me much.'

'Look, Inspector, instead of pissin' around comin' here, you wanna take a drive over to the new casino what's opened up in Camas.'

'Now why would I want to do that, Diego?'

'Front for our Russkie friends, ain't it.'

Velázquez was beginning to wonder if Diego Blanco might

have a point. A potentially Russian victim, the Russian mafia in the Camas casino—assuming what the man had just said was true—added to the way the city's criminal underworld had taken on a certain Russian tint in places over the past few months, caused the Inspector Jefe to wonder if this latest killing might possibly be a mafia hit.

He slipped down off his stool and said, 'I gotta go.'

'So soon?'

'Don't worry—I'll be back.'

The midday sun was doing its worst and the air conditioner in Velázquez's Alfa Romeo had chosen now of all times to pack up, so that his shirt was wringing wet by the time he pulled into the car park outside of the new casino in Camas.

It was a large white building with an elegant façade, and looked like some ritzy hotel. Beyond you could see the dry hills baking under the molten sun in the distance. The Inspector Jefe climbed out of his car and made a dash for the shade, then headed over to the tongue of red carpet that protruded from the entrance. The doorman, who looked more like Cary Grant than Arnie Schwarzenegger, smiled and welcomed him in with a velvety *'Buenas tardes, señor,'* as the electronic doors parted and closed behind him. Velázquez passed through the reception area, a large atrium with a fountain in the middle of it and a glass ceiling, which led into the gambling area.

The place was all red plush, leather and mahogany and, as had been the case with Diego Blanco's club, appeared to be doing a reasonable trade despite the time of day. Some people, Velázquez observed, just seemed to live to drink and gamble. Made you wonder where they got their money from. Not from gambling— the casinos made sure of that.

Most of them seemed to be Spanish or South American, with a sprinkling of Chinese. But he couldn't see anybody who looked Russian. Nor did he hear any Russian accents. Which might not mean a thing, of course. You could own a place, after all, without even visiting it.

Noticing a tall elegant blonde woman in a blue trouser suit, who looked like she was there to keep an eye on the tables, he went over and introduced himself, said he wanted to see the manager. 'Is there a problem?' she asked.

'No, just get me the manager.' Velázquez held out his ID.

'Please come with me.' Velázquez followed her back out to the reception area, then waited while she went behind the desk, picked up a phone and called her boss. She said something into the receiver that Velázquez didn't hear, then hung up before she turned back to him and said, 'He'll be down in a moment, *señor*, if you'd just like to wait.'

Velázquez thanked the woman. She offered him a deprecating smile: it was her pleasure. Perhaps the Inspector Jefe would like to make himself comfortable on one of the easy chairs over by the wall? No, it was quite all right, he would just as soon stand.

If the Russian mafia really were behind this parade of elegance and manners, Velázquez thought, then there was an awful lot a common hoodlum like Diego Blanco could learn from the way they ran things. The place reeked of money. More of the stuff than Velázquez could even begin to imagine. And wealth like that meant power. No wonder Diego Blanco was getting so edgy. Unless, Velázquez thought, the man had been bullshitting him. He wouldn't put it past him.

The manager, Rodriguez, came striding towards Velázquez, every inch the boss in his elegant grey suit and white shirt, a serious look on his broad face. 'Good morning, Inspector uh...'

'Inspector *Jefe* Velázquez.' He flashed his ID again.

Rodriguez looked at it, frowned. 'Is there some problem, Inspector Jefe?'

'I wonder if you could give me a few minutes of your time?'

'Certainly... please come this way.'

Velázquez followed the man up a few steps and along a red-plush-lined corridor, then through a panelled door at the end into a room full of TV screens. There was a large desk done in mahogany. Rodriguez sat down behind it and Velázquez sat facing him. Rodriguez flipped open the humidor. 'Cigar…?'

Velázquez shook his head. 'Little early in the day.'

'So how can I help you?'

'Can you tell me who the main shareholders are for this place?'

'Company by the name of Waterford Incorporated owns the lion's share.'

'How much would that be?'

'Ninety-five percent, to be precise.'

'And where is this Waterford Incorporated based?'

'New York.'

'Can you tell me anything else about them?'

Rodriguez shrugged. 'Not really,' he said. 'I'm the manager of this place, but there's nothing in my job description that says I need to know anything about the shareholders' business interests… I mean, I'm just here to ensure the place runs efficiently on a day to day basis. I manage the staff and make sure they're doing their jobs properly, that nobody's on the take and none of the punters are cheating.'

'It's not owned by Russians, then?'

Rodriguez's dark brows rose in a look of confused enquiry. 'Russians…? Certainly not to the best of my knowledge… *Waterford Incorporated* doesn't have much of a Russian ring to it, does it? And they're based in New York, so no, I can't see it being a Russian company, can you?'

Velázquez took his leave of the man and headed out to his car. The heat was stifling, and he could feel the sweat dripping down his back as he climbed in behind the wheel. He drove back into the city to pay a call on his old friend, Jaime Arrese, in Nervion.

A big man with salt-and-pepper beard and a bulging headland of gut that protruded over his belt, Jaime Arrese seemed happy to see Velázquez, as ever. 'Neither of us are getting any slimmer,

Jaime,' Velázquez said. 'What happened to your plans to start going to the gym?'

'Why do we always agree to start a new health regime when we're out together in some bar in the early hours with a bellyful of gin in us?'

'Probably,' Velázquez said, 'because we're out in some bar in the early hours with a bellyful of gin in us...'

Jaime laughed and slumped in his chair, behind a desk crowded with piles of folders, a second desk at right angles to it playing home to his computer. Overhead a propeller fan was fighting a losing battle against the incessant heat. He gestured towards the vacant chair and said, 'Take a load off.'

Velázquez perched on the edge of the chair and looked at Jaime. 'I hope I'm not disturbing you...?'

'You're keeping me from my work,' Jaime said. 'But you're not disturbing me... Rather a relief to have an excuse to come up for a few minutes from under this mountain of paper.'

Jaime always said this, even though he was in actual fact one of the most hard-working and successful notaries in all Seville.

'Work,' Velázquez said. 'Can't stand doing it, but we can't leave it alone...'

'Rather like women...' Jaime waved his hand: they would save that conversation for their next drinking bout. 'So how can I help you?'

'I need to find out who owns Waterford Incorporated.'

'I can look into it for you,' Jaime said. 'When do you need to know by?'

'Tomorrow too soon?'

'Shouldn't be.'

'Great.' Velázquez got to his feet. 'I'll treat you to lunch at the Rinconcillo at two, then.'

He was driving through a narrow cobbled street in the Old Quarter, when his mobile began to ring. He answered it, taking one hand off the wheel. 'Boss? It's me,' came Gajardo's voice.

'What's new, José?' Velázquez stopped for a red light.

'We've got an ID for the latest vic... Looks like you hit the nail on the head, Boss—name was Vladimir Vorosky. Científicos've finished examining the crime scene, and a passport for the vic was found there... Could be Russian mafia, after all.'

'We still need proof of that, of course.'

'Assuming you're right and it's a turf war, then the killer's either gotta be another Russian, or—'

'Some local hoodlum.'

'Diego Blanco's the first name to spring to mind, Boss.'

'Yes, well you can't lift a stone in this city without finding evidence of his influence under it, I know. But even so, we don't want to jump the gun, José,' Velázquez said. 'Case of keeping on doing the legwork and seeing what we can turn up... You checked yet to see if this Vorosky character had any form?'

'No, he didn't.'

'Manage to find out how long he'd been in Seville?'

'Moved into his current address back in March.'

'Any idea where he was before that?'

'Afraid not.'

'He have a NIE?'

'Nope.'

'If he came over from Russia in March, then for all we know he could be wanted by the police over there.'

'So what d'you want me to do, Boss?'

'You got the man's passport with you?'

'Have indeed.'

'Take a look inside and see where he was born,' Velázquez said.

'Hang on a sec.'

Velázquez listened to Gajardo breathing down the line, then the Subinspector said, 'In Moscow, Boss.'

'Date of birth?'

'Tenth of October nineteen seventy three.'

'Right, well, there's a fair bit to go on, José... Why don't you try and call the cops in Moscow and see if they've ever heard of him. Get someone to make the call for you who can speak Russkie.'

'Where am I going to find a Russian speaker?'

'Use your initiative, José,' Velázquez said. 'Speak to some colleagues, find out the last time somebody had call to use a translator or interpreter... Failing that, try the university.'

'Okay, Boss.'

'And if it turns out the cops in Moscow are familiar with this Vladimir Vorosky, then we'll need to know what he was doing over there and who his associates were.'

'Because the chances are some of them are over here now, you're thinking, right?'

'Exactly... I've been making enquiries concerning the new casino over in Camas. Rumour going round it's owned by the Russians.'

'As in the Russian mafia, you mean?'

By the time Velazquez reached Forensics, Gómez was already at the dissecting table, cutting up the latest murder victim.

'Got anything for me yet, Juan?'

'There are traces of FDR in the victim's hair that suggest a different gun from the one used on the two priests.'

'Any foreign DNA found?'

'Afraid not.'

Velázquez wasn't surprised; he had already concluded that the victim was probably shot in his sleep. The killer wouldn't have needed to get close enough to leave any DNA.

The Inspector Jefe made to leave, but Gómez called after him: 'Hey, Luis...'

Velázquez stopped and turned. 'What?'

'You should stop worrying so much about Pe being a *torera*.'

'Huh...?'

'She's a natural,' Gómez said. 'And whenever anyone's that good at something, there's only one thing you can do.'

'And what's that?'

'Just let them carry on doing it.'

Velázquez called his team together for a briefing at the *Jefatura* at two thirty that afternoon.

'Okay, so we've now got three bodies,' he said, turning to the whiteboard behind him and pointing to the victims' mug shots. 'Same *modus operandi* was used on both priests, and the same kind of bullet, suggesting of course that the same gun was used in both killings—very possibly a .38 Smith & Wesson.'

'Different MO for the Russian, though, Boss,' Jorge Serrano cut in.

'Absolutely, and traces of FDR were found in Vladimir Vorosky's hair that suggest a different firearm was used on him.'

Agente Pérez said, 'So are we saying we're after two killers, Boss, or what?'

'Could well be.'

'Or it could be the same killer using a different MO to make us fall into the trap of thinking that,' Gajardo reasoned.

'That's true, too.' Velázquez gave his chin a thoughtful scratch. 'Okay, so where do we go from here? Anyone got any ideas they'd like to contribute?'

Silence.

'Let's go over what we've managed to learn so far again, shall we?' Velázquez said. 'Who's going to help me out?'

More silence.

'You've been quiet today, Jorge, so perhaps you can tell us something?'

Agente Serrano's blue eyes narrowed. 'Tell you what exactly, Boss?'

'Just recap for us what we've learned so far, to help us focus our thoughts… maybe that way we'll be able to see a line of enquiry we've overlooked.'

'Both priests served at the same church, the Iglesia de Jesus del Gran Poder, for one. First vic seems to've called an escort agency and asked them to send a rent boy over—'

'Who's just come out of a coma,' Javier Merino cut in, 'after an attempt was made on his life.'

'Using my car, which appears to have been stolen with that purpose in mind,' Velázquez said.

'So Ochoa's the fall guy,' Pérez reasoned. 'He was set up.'

'Exactly,' Velázquez concurred.

'Who by, is the question,' Jorge Serrano suggested.

Sara Pérez said, 'Have we warned Father Antonio that he could be next?'

Velázquez nodded. 'I've spoken to him and warned him of the need to take every precaution.'

'What do we know about this last vic, Boss,' Pérez asked, 'other than what you've just told us?'

'Maybe the Subinspector can help us there...' Velázquez turned his head to look at Gajardo. 'You manage to talk to any detectives over in Moscow yet, José?'

'About an hour ago, Boss.'

'Got anything to tell us?'

'The detective I spoke to said he'd never heard of a Vladimir Vorosky.'

'The passport could have been fake—did you send the man a mug shot?'

'That did occur to me, Boss, so I faxed over a copy. But the face didn't ring any bells either.'

'Which doesn't necessarily mean he wasn't mixed up in something over in Moscow, of course.' Velázquez scratched his nose. 'Anyway, the rest of you may be interested to know that there's a casino recently been opened out in Camas, and I've had a tip-off that the Russian mafia has a large stake in it... Would make sense, given that we know the Russians have gained a foothold in the city's criminal Underworld over the past year or so.'

'Maybe this could've been some kind of hit then, Boss—is that what you're saying?' Javier Merino said.

Pérez nodded in agreement. 'Maybe it was an internal power battle of some kind... You know what these gangster types are like.'

'No,' Jorge Serrano grinned, 'can't say I do, Sara... What are they like?'

'All got dicks bigger than their brains, and egos bigger than both.'

Velázquez went out with his team, and didn't clock off until just after 2 a.m. By that time, he was feeling tired and in need of a fix. So badly in need of one, in fact, that he drove at nearly double the speed limit most of the way back across town, and pulled up with a great screech of rubber on Calle Teodosio.

As he climbed out of the car, he was vaguely conscious of the sound of a brass band playing somewhere away in the distance, a sound that was as much a part of Seville as the scent of oranges. The bands would practise all the year round, in preparation for Holy Week, and they always played the same tender, mournful music, so that you ended up hearing it and not hearing it. But it was always there, serving as a sort of eternal soundtrack against which the city went about its business each day. You heard it at the bullfights, too, the trumpets working to produce a proud blare at times; other times they could touch your heart with a soulful lament.

Velázquez dashed into the building, his shoes slipping on the tiles as he hurried through the lobby and ran up the stairs to the flat. No sign of Pe, so he looked in the bedroom—and found her in there fast asleep. Then he went into the kitchen and injected himself with methadone.

It didn't give you the same kind of hit that you got from the real thing, nowhere near—less a wild bull charging through your veins than a playful pony; but at least it took away the feeling of nausea and the clammy, fluey sensation.

And it was a step in the right direction, he told himself. The first step towards kicking the habit altogether.

Fingers crossed...

CHAPTER 13

The following morning, Velazquez stood looking out his office window while he drank the muck the coffee the machine downstairs turned out. The view of Seville was splendid: the city's many church spires punctuated the skyline like so many notes on a musical score—one whose dominant chord was the Giralda, which glowed like a jewelled challis in the distance. Below, in the foreground, the Guadalquivir snaked its way through the heart of the city like a golden serpent, its bridges crawling with people and traffic. It was a typically fine summer morning; the sun was pouring its golden honey out of a Wedgewood sky with mild forbearance, as if to allow the city and its residents a little more time to recover from their nocturnal revelries before it began to burn with a vengeance. Just the sort of view you'd want to be able to look out on from your office window. And anybody who'd been watching the Inspector Jefe del Grupo de Homicidios would no doubt have presumed he was taking a minute or two out to appreciate the visual delights that Seville had to offer—but Velazquez was taken up instead with an interior film of the case running in his head.

He tossed the empty plastic cup into a rubbish bin and then spent the next couple of hours at his desk writing up his report. Dull but essential work, he reminded Merino and Serrano. 'Trouble with you two is,' he said, 'you've both been watching too many cop movies. Wanna be Mel Gibson and Dirty fucking Harry, the pair of you... But what you've got to learn is that a large part of police work is concerned with collecting and processing data, are you with me?'

'Yes, Boss,' Serrano and Merino replied in unison.

'Good, so get on with writing your frigging reports, then,

and don't whinge about it. *Coj-ooo-nes!'*

Gajardo of course knew better than to complain; as for Agente Pérez, she just did everything that was asked of her in double-quick time. And she did it all well. *Bloody* well. And then she'd do a few other things that you hadn't even asked her to do, things that would all turn out to be intelligent and useful. But it wasn't fair on Serrano and Merino to compare them to her. Serrano was actually a pretty good cop. And Merino would probably be a decent cop, too, given time. They just weren't great cops.

But Sara Pérez had all the makings of becoming a great cop.

Jaime Arrese was already there, standing at the horseshoe-shaped bar, when Velázquez showed at the Rinconcillo that afternoon. Fat and elegant as ever, with his smart pinstriped suit and burgundy tie, neatly trimmed beard, and perfectly layered hair, the Inspector Jefe's friend hadn't changed much these past few years. Behind him pigs' legs hung from hooks above the wooden counter, where the day's menu sat, chalked up on a blackboard. Never one to waste time when it came to eating, Jaime had already demolished a variety of tapas. He grinned at Velázquez and they shook hands.

'You know something, Luis, the owners of Waterford Incorporated are Russian. Fancy that.'

'Can't say I'm surprised… but thanks for finding out for me, and at such short notice.'

Jaime took one of the *boquerones* from the small dish at his elbow and popped it into his mouth. 'These are *good*, I must say.' He had a gourmand's appetite to match his girth.

Velázquez ordered *albondigas* and opted for the house Rioja.

'What's all this about the Russians anyway?' Jaime asked.

'Seems they're making their presence felt in the city's criminal Underworld.' Velázquez popped a meat ball into his mouth. It was hot and tasted good. He washed it down with a mouthful of Rioja and changed the subject.

'How's Monica?'

'Marriage is on the rocks, to tell you the truth, Luis.'

'No.'

'My own fault… she caught me cheating with my secretary.'

'*Joder!*'

'My father made a lifelong habit of it.' Jaime sighed. 'Way it was back then. Old boy went at it like a bull from what I gather, but Mother never kicked up a fuss.'

Maybe she should have, Velázquez thought. 'Suppose it was different in those days.'

'Too bloody right it was, Luis.'

'How bad is it?'

Jaime shot Velázquez a pained look. 'Monica's saying she wants a divorce.'

'Can't you try and make it up to her?'

'Pulling out all the stops, Luis… but it doesn't seem to be working.'

Velázquez demolished another meat ball. 'I'm truly sorry to hear that, Jaime… I dunno what to say.'

'Nothing *to* say.' Jaime shrugged. 'Thing about these sorts of situations is, they can go either way, you know?'

Velázquez had gone out with Monica once, but she'd told him she didn't want to marry a cop. Actually he hadn't been looking for a wife anyway, but he never mentioned this since she didn't ask for his thoughts on the subject. Next time he saw her, she was going steady with Jaime.

Velázquez's mobile rang. He worked it up out of his pocket.

'*Hola*?'

'Me, Boss,' came the familiar voice of Subinspector Gajardo. 'Traced the reg of the vehicle that drove at you outside the hospital to a car that was stolen two days ago over in Bami.'

'Surprise, surprise.' Velázquez sipped his wine. 'Any more news?'

'There's this guy walked into the station yesterday and made a complaint about a brothel out in Camas.'

'Camas, huh…?'

'What I was thinking, Boss… what with you mentioning the casino over there.'

'Go on.'

'Seems it's run by Russians—the brothel, I mean… girls are kept in rooms over there, the bloke reckons, and not allowed out.'

'What's the guy's interest in it?'

'He's in love with one of the girls there… wants her to leave and set up house with him.'

'Does the girl want to leave?'

'Sounds like she's scared,' Gajardo said. 'She says the Russian who runs the brothel would have both of them killed… But the guy's willing to take the risk.'

'And wants us to help him get her out?'

'Or shut the place down.'

'Sounds like he's got some *cojones*.'

'Have to give him that… not so sure whether he's got much up top, though.'

'Spoken to him yet?'

'No, I got all this from the officer he made the complaint to.'

'Torres?'

'That's the one.'

Velázquez chewed on what Gajardo had just told him for a moment.

'You want me to go over to the brothel, Boss?'

'And do what…?'

'That's what I'm wondering.'

'When you build a house it's best not to start with the roof, José,' Velázquez said. 'Might end up getting the guy killed… and the girl would probably take a beating.'

'There is that risk, I suppose.'

'Find the guy who made the complaint, bring him in and we'll question him.'

'Don't have a name or address for him, I'm afraid.'

'How on earth did that come about?'

'Man said his piece to the desk sergeant then scarpered when he was asked for his deets.'

'Great help.'

'Sorry, Boss.'

'Not your fault, José,' Velázquez said.

'What do you want me to do now?'

'We need to find this Russian guy… Get Torres to work with the police artist to produce a portrait so we can get a photo fit made up.'

Velázquez arrived at the *Jefatura*, some forty minutes later. His office had been turned into an artist's studio: sketch pads, pencils, ink, charcoal. Torres the desk sergeant was standing over the police artist, looking strained. The artist was sketching feverishly. Torres leaned over him to get a closer look. 'No, his eyes are a little closer together.'

Velazquez glanced down at the sketch as he strolled past them on his way to his desk. A face was taking shape, slowly.

'Forehead wasn't so broad,' continued Torres.

'What was he, a Neanderthal?' quipped Velazquez, glancing out of the window.

With a show of theatrical patience, the artist rubbed out the bits that were wrong. Torres grimaced. 'Ears were bigger, too.'

Gajardo came in, carrying a cup of coffee from the machine downstairs. 'Would've got you one if I'd known you were here, Boss,' the Subinspector said. 'Comisario Alonso was looking for you a short time ago… told me to ask you to go'n see him in his office soon as you arrive.'

'Better go and see what he wants, I suppose.'

'Chin stuck out a little more,' said Torres, as Velazquez made his way out.

Velázquez ran up the stairs and knocked on the Comisario's door. 'Come,' boomed the Comisario's voice. Velázquez entered to find him standing over by the window, looking down over the city.

Comisario Alonso turned and his eyes flashed with anger when he saw who it was. A shortish man with plenty of belly, his physique resembled an enormous egg. And one look at the man's face was enough to tell Velázquez he'd been drinking the bad milk. 'Inspector Jefe,' he said, 'what in hell's name has been going on?'

'Chief…?'

'Three men murdered and a fourth in hospital after being hit by an old Alfa Romeo Nuova Giulietta… I'm told you drive an Alfa Romeo Nuova Giulietta, too, Inspector Jefe… And the first four digits on the registration plate just happen to match the first four digits on the reg on your car…'

'I know, but I can explain—'

'I haven't finished, Velázquez… I've just been talking to a distraught mother who wants to have you charged with attempted murder—or murder one if her son ends up dying.'

'But Comisario—'

'You're off the case—'

'But haven't you heard the news, Chief—Ramón Ochoa's recovered consciousness, and he knows it wasn't me that tried to kill him.'

The Comisario's brows bunched in a frown as he took on board what he'd just been told. Then he looked at Velázquez and said, 'Any idea who did?'

'Whoever it was, he tried to frame me.'

'Why would anyone want to do that, Inspector Jefe?'

'Simple, Comisario,' Velázquez said. 'To try and get me taken off the case… The killer tried to frame Ramón Ochoa for killing the two priests, and then he tried to frame me for killing Ochoa… that way the killer must've thought he'd get away scot-free–case closed, end of story.'

'So you still think it's just the one killer we're after, do you?'

'So far as the two priests are concerned, yes.'

'What about the Russian?'

'Still trying to find a link.'

'Any leads?'

'A number of them, as it happens, Chief.'

The Comisario fixed Velázquez with his stony, unimpressed look. 'So you haven't just been running around in circles on this one, then?'

'Not at all.'

'That's funny... I'd rather picked up the impression you were chasing your own tail and getting nowhere fast.'

'Far from it... We've been making fast progress on a couple of lines of enquiry.'

'So you will be making an arrest soon—that what you're telling me?'

'Only a matter of time.'

'Time's the thing we're running out of fast, Inspector Jefe. Do I make myself clear?'

'We've all be working round the clock on this one.'

Comisario Alonso scratched his bald head. 'Okay,' he said. 'I'll give you one more chance, Velázquez—but you'd better make sure you don't screw up this time... because if you do, I'll have your ass in the proverbial sling.'

'Thanks, Chief—I won't screw up.'

'I hope not for your sake, because it's your career that's on the line... Do I make myself understood?'

As soon as the portrait was finished, the Inspector Jefe had a number of photocopies run off. He pinned a few up in the office and around the building, then sent a copy off to the tekkies so they could make a photo fit, told them it was urgent, and they had it ready before he assembled his team in the office for another briefing at nine the following morning. 'A Russian's come into the *Jefatura* complaining that his girlfriend is being held captive in a brothel in Camas. Says she's forced to work there against her will,' he began, then handed out the photocopies. 'The picture I've just given you all is a close likeness, according to Oficial Torres. So you can take it out with you and show it to people, because we need to find this guy and bring him in and talk to him.'

'What for exactly, Boss?' Agente Serrano wanted to know. 'I mean, what's his connection with the murders?'

'Maybe there is no direct connection.'

Serrano looked confused.

'I've had a tip-off that the Russian mafia owns the new casino over in Camas, as well as the *puticlub*,' Velázquez said. 'What's more, my source also seems to think that Vladimir Vorosky had links to the Russian mafia, and although we have no evidence to back this theory up at present it does seem like a reasonable one–or certainly one that's worth investigating... So if we can find the girlfriend of this other Russian who spoke to Torres, and get her out of the *puticlub*, then she might be able to offer us information about her Russian employers that we could use to make things difficult for them... Might even be able to get the *puticlub* closed down.'

'How's this gonna help us get closer to finding out who killed Vorosky, though?' Gajardo wondered aloud.

'These organizations work like a chain... the men at the top get the people at the bottom do their dirty work for them.'

'How they stop us from getting at them,' Serrano put in.

'But their system isn't foolproof. No system ever is. Look at the way the FBI closed down the Five Families over in America. And how did they do it? Quite simple, really. They got dirt on people lower down the chain, then gave them a simple choice: talk or go away for a long time.'

'And they all started talking,' Pérez said. 'Or enough of them did for the FBI to be able to bring down the Five Families, anyway... I read about it.'

'Exactly,' Velázquez nodded. 'So if we can talk to this man

and perhaps make contact with his girlfriend, and get her out, then she may be able to tell us something that we can use... Because she'll be scared, remember, so we'll be in a position to be able to offer her our help and protection—her and her boyfriend.'

'You're hoping she might be able to give us some dirt on one or two of the links in the chain, Boss, you're saying, right?' Gajardo said. 'And then if we can charge a couple of guys, we offer them a deal—'

'They tell us who killed Vorosky,' Pérez cut in, 'and they get a reduced sentence...'

'Worth a shot, anyway,' said Velázquez.

'But where are we are going to start looking for this man whose girlfriend's in the brothel, Boss?' Serrano wanted to know. 'I mean, he could be anywhere in the city.'

'He's a Russian with bad Spanish, so the chances are he's taking lessons.'

'You're thinking language schools, right?'

'Exactly. And don't just ask the teachers or the people who run the schools, but talk to any Russian students—and Russians in general—you can find as well. If you show enough people the man's portrait someone out there's gotta know where we can find him. Okay? Any questions? No? Good, so let's get our booties out there and see what we can find.'

Velázquez put his jacket on and took the lift down to the car park with Pérez and Gajardo. 'Pe's got another *corrida*,' the Inspector Jefe said, 'so I wonder if you'd cover for me again, José?'

'Of course, Boss.'

'Just a question of keeping in touch with Sara here, and Serrano and Merino, and making sure they all know what they're supposed to be doing. You can contact me on my mobile if you need to, or if any of you find the man we're looking for.' Velázquez had been putting in eighteen-hour shifts or more on average for a long time, yet he still felt guilty. But there was no way he was about to miss one of Pe's *corridas* if he could help it. He knew how much her bullfighting meant to her, and knew how disappointed she would be if he failed to show.

Velázquez parted from the other two officers in the underground car park, then drove over to the Escuela de Idiomas on Avenida Dr. Fedriani. He flashed his ID at the receptionist, a pleasant-looking and rather plump brunette in her thirties, and showed her the portrait of the man he was looking for. She shook her head. 'Sorry, I've never seen him in here.'

'He's Russian.'

'We do have a couple of Russian students, so you could always try talking to them.'

'Are they in the school at the moment?'

'No, they come in tomorrow.'

'You got their phone numbers and addresses?'

'Yes, I'll just look them up a moment.'

The woman tapped at a few keys on her computer, then found pen and paper. 'Here they are.' Velázquez thanked her, and looked at what she had written as he walked back to his car.

Before starting the engine up, he called Gajardo and passed the names, numbers and addresses on to him. 'Talk to them and see what you can find out, José.'

'Okay, Boss… and please send Pe my regards. I hope she gets some good bulls this evening.'

'I hope so, too.'

More than anything, though, he just hoped and prayed that she'd get through the evening unscathed.

Chapter 14

As he got closer to Torremolinos, Velázquez began to get more and more nervous. Sweat beaded on his forehead, formed battalions that marched on his eyebrows and down the bridge of his nose. What if Pe doesn't come home with me tonight? he thought. What if the bull ends up winning this time?

Of course the poor beast was destined to lose whatever the outcome... but what if it took Pe with him?

Velázquez felt himself breathing the dangerous air of high anxiety as he pulled up outside of the bullring. He had time for a quick drink to settle his nerves before the *corrida* started, so he entered a bar and had the barman pour him a large Scotch on the rocks. But the Scotch only made him sweat all the more. He washed it down with a glass of water, then had the barman uncork him a bottle of Rioja to take.

He showed the man on the gate his complimentary ticket and went and took his seat by the *barrera*, where he had a bird's-eye view. The sun was beating down with all the spite of some particularly vicious Grand Inquisitor, and Velázquez put the bottle to his lips and swigged. It tasted good and, this being a third-rate ring, there was no need for social niceties.

He glanced around: the place was barely half full. Only the diehards would come to a place like this to see a bullfight. The diehards and those with nothing better to do. The trumpets started up, and Pe strolled out into the bullring.

Velázquez felt his stomach turn over. At least driving down here, he'd needed to be in control of his car, and that had given him something to think about. But now that he was reduced to playing the role of passive spectator, he was a mass of jangling nerves.

He swigged the Rioja and mopped his forehead with his

handkerchief, as Pe and her *peones* went to work. Then he felt a hand grip him in the belly and twist, and was forced to get up and make a dash up the steps and out into the concourse, in search of the gents'.

He passed a difficult few minutes in one of the cubicles there, but was feeling a little more human by the time he emerged. He washed his hands, poured cold water over his head, and was just enjoying the feel of the water running down the back of his scalp, and over his face, when he heard loud cries coming from outside.

Something had happened.

His heart hammered out a nasty punk-rock beat as he hurried back into the stand. By now the crowd was on its feet, and... *Oh my God, no!* Pe was being carried from the ring. Her head had fallen to the side, and she appeared to be unconscious. Velázquez ran down the steps, then climbed up onto the *barrera* and jumped down into the *callejon*. A man ran over to him. 'I am sorry, *señor*, you cannot stay here.'

'I'm Pe Naranjo's partner,' he replied. 'We live together.'

'Come with me.'

Velázquez followed the man around the side of the ring, and into the infirmary, where a doctor was already attending to Pe. Her tunic was soaked with blood by now. Velázquez rushed to her side and the doctor gave him a sharp look. 'I'm her partner,' Velázquez said. Then he took Pe's hand in his and gave it a tender squeeze.

'It's all right, Pe,' he told her. 'You're gonna be okay.' He had no idea whether this was true—not that she would have heard a word he'd said anyway, because she was clearly out cold. He could see from the amount of blood she'd lost that the wound must be serious.

The doctor said, 'She needs to go to hospital–there's no time to lose.'

Tears rushed to Velázquez's eyes as the ambulance men came

in and carried her off on a stretcher. I knew this was going to happen sooner or later, he thought. It was just a matter of time. He remembered the thought that had crossed his mind as he'd driven down from Seville: *what if Pe doesn't come home with me tonight?*

The stretcher bearers disappeared with Pe into the back of the ambulance. He went to climb in the back, but the ambulance driver put out his hand to stop him. 'Sorry, *señor*, but nobody's allowed inside with her.'

'But I'm her partner... we live together.'

'I'm sorry. I'm taking her to the Hospital Clinico, in Málaga... you can visit her there.' The man closed the doors, and then the ambulance drove away.

Velázquez ran out and climbed into his car, but by the time he'd started it up the ambulance was nowhere to be seen. The ambulance man had said they were taking her to the Hospital Clinico in Malaga. Velázquez didn't know the hospital. He didn't know the city very well, either, come to that, although he had been there a few times. But he knew it wasn't all that far away. Just a ten or fifteen-minute drive along the coast, he thought, as he headed out of the car park. And the hospital shouldn't be hard to find. Just a case of keeping an eye out for the road signs, he told himself, as he headed up to the next roundabout, then joined the motorway and really put his put down.

He wondered why the driver hadn't taken Pe to a hospital in Torremolinos. Maybe they didn't have one. Torremolinos was just a small coastal resort, after all, while Málaga was a proper city. Besides, he thought, even if there was a hospital in Torremolinos, the one in Málaga would be bigger and better equipped.

The traffic was thick as he joined the busy road that runs into the city; he turned off at the sign for the Hospital Clinico, and found himself heading through the middle-class *barrio* of

Teatinos with its broad streets and modern apartment blocks. Then he saw the hospital, a big white building, and drove into the car park, parked any old how, jumped out and ran over to the exit and in through the automatic doors. 'I need Emergencies,' he told the man behind the reception counter. The man asked for his name and *carné*.

Velázquez flashed his ID. 'I've haven't got time for that,' he said. 'Just tell me where Emergencies is.'

'Out through that door, then turn left and left again.'

Velázquez dashed off, and seconds later was in Emergencies. 'I'm looking for Penelope Naranjo,' he told the man behind the reception desk. 'The ambulance driver said he was bringing her here.'

'We've got somebody's just been brought in after a car crash...'

'Penelope Naranjo's a bullfighter... She took a goring at a *corrida* down in Torremolinos.'

The man shook his head. 'Haven't had any bullfighters in here this evening.'

Velázquez found a doctor and asked him if he'd seen Pe.

No.

He asked several of the nurses on duty.

No.

His heart was working up a frenetic drum solo in his chest.

Figuring the ambulance driver could have changed his mind about where to take her, Velázquez tried calling the other hospitals in Málaga.

Pe wasn't at any of them.

He called all the hospitals in the region, stretching all the way from Nerja to Marbella.

Nothing.

Velázquez wondered if he'd been tricked.

Told himself not to jump to conclusions.

Trouble with this job, you got into the habit of expecting the worst.

He returned to the reception desk, showed the man sitting behind it his ID. 'I need you to contact all the ambulance drivers in the area, and find out if one of them is carrying Pe Naranjo. She's a bullfighter and she was badly gored at a *corrida* earlier this evening in Torremolinos... they put her in the back of an ambulance, and the driver told me he was bringing her here.'

'So maybe the ambulance is on its way.'

'It left the bullring before I did, and I've been here over fifteen minutes now,' Velázquez said. 'Doesn't take that long to get here... it's only a short drive.'

The man told him to wait a moment, then went off somewhere. When he returned, shortly afterwards, he looked at Velázquez and shook his head. 'Isn't any ambulance out there carrying a Pe Naranjo.' The man shrugged. 'There's a record of an ambulance having been called out to the *plaza de toros* in Torremolinos to collect a lady bullfighter who'd been gored, but there was no bullfighter there when the ambulance arrived.'

'What do you mean...?'

'According to what I've just been told, she'd already left.'

Someone's taken her, Velázquez thought.

Question is, *who..*?

Velázquez went back out into the car park and climbed into the Alfa Romeo. As he turned the key in the ignition, a huge tsunami of solid emotion racked his entire being, and he began to sob.

When he'd cried himself out, he dried his eyes with the backs of his hands and set off. Minutes later, he was on the motorway heading for Seville. He drove with his foot down all the way, his mind so full of what had happened to Pe that he was only dimly aware of what he was doing. He was operating on automatic pilot, and it was probably a minor miracle that he managed to get back to Seville without having a crash, seeing how fast he was driving. Then as soon as he got home, he found the bottle of Scotch and poured himself a large one. Sat on the sofa taking sips from it, and going over what had happened in his mind.

Velázquez sat there like that for some time, oscillating between rage and tearfulness. He poured himself another large one. Drank it quickly and refilled the glass, then paced the room endlessly, gulping down his Scotch. Every so often he'd notice his glass was empty, and stop to give himself another refill. Time had stopped. Pe had been taken. There was only one thought in his head: how to get her back.

His mobile began to vibrate and slither over the sofa, like a sidewinder over the desert sand. He snatched it up. '*Hola?*'

A voice Velázquez didn't recognize said, 'We have your girlfriend, Inspector Jefe.'

'Is she all right?'

'Yes, she's is perfectly safe.'

'Who are you? Why have you taken her?'

'All in good time.'

The man's accent had a Russian twang to it.

'Listen, you crazy son of the great whore, she was badly gored! She's going to die if she doesn't get expert medical attention!'

'There's no need to worry on that score, I can assure you. And for your information, I am not a crazy maniac but a businessman. Do as I say and you will get your precious girlfriend back unharmed. It's your choice.'

'But she needs to be in a hospital... the wound could infect.'

'I told you, there's no need to worry... our surgeon has patched her up like new. Your girlfriend is just fine.'

Velázquez swallowed.

'We'll be in touch,' the man said. 'And listen, Inspector Jefe, you need to play this one alone if you ever want to see your girlfriend alive again, you understand? No cops, okay?' The man let out an evil little chuckle. 'Except you, of course.'

'Okay, no cops... But why did you take her? Is this your pathetic and stupid way of trying to get at me?'

The caller had already hung up.

Now what?

We'll be in touch. They must want something from him… and presumably it wouldn't be long before he found out what it was.

Velázquez was angrier than he'd ever been in his life.

He looked at his mobile and cursed. *'Joder!'*

Then it began to ring again.

'Diga?'

But this time it was only Gajardo. Velázquez's heart sank.

'Nothing much to report, Boss,' the Subinspector said. 'None of the Russian students recognized the face in the portrait… But I just thought I'd call to ask how Pe got on in the *corrida?*'

'I'm living out a nightmare, José,' Velázquez told him, and explained.

They both went quiet for a moment and then Gajardo said, 'So what do we do now?'

'Nothing *to* do except wait for the guy to call again, I guess.'

'He say when to expect his call?'

'No, just that he'd be in touch… and he said they had a doctor of their own looking after Pe, and that she's going to be fine.'

Silence.

Velázquez took a swig of his Scotch.

'What d'you reckon they want, Boss?'

'That's what I've been sitting here asking myself.'

'What makes you so sure it's the Russians?'

'Man's accent, for one thing,' Velázquez said. 'Besides, who else can it be?'

'Could be Diego Blanco, and he gets a guy with a Russian accent to make the call, just to put you off the scent.'

'Possibility, I suppose.'

'You at home now, Boss?'

'Sí.'

'Want me to come over?'

'No point.'

'Anything I can help you with?'

'No, I'll get back to you as soon as the kidnappers call again,' Velázquez said. 'Listen, José, not a word about this to anyone, okay? I'm gonna handle it my way.'

'Sure that's the best way to go about it?'

'I'm sure,' Velázquez said. 'You may as well grab some sleep. We're both gonna need to be fresh and wide awake tomorrow.'

They said *buenas noches* and hung up.

It had to be the mafia behind it, he thought. In other words, either the Russians or Diego Blanco's outfit.

Who else would kidnap a police detective's girlfriend?

Why had they taken her, though…?

Obvious, he thought. To get at me.

Where could they have taken her?

She could be anywhere. There was no way he could even begin to search.

Velázquez's head began to spin. He took deep breaths, and willed himself to calm down and get a grip.

He had to remind himself that he was an experienced police detective: Inspector Jefe del Grupo de Homicidios, no less. But somehow all his experience seemed to count for nothing now.

He'd never had to work on a case in which someone he loved was taken from him. Velázquez realized that his own emotions were his worst enemy right now. The very love that he felt for Pe was working against him. He needed to approach this case with the same cool professionalism that he was known for, and he needed to eliminate the personal element.

He mopped the sweat from his forehead; then, feeling again as if somebody had put their fist into his belly and proceeded to squeeze and twist his guts, he dashed to the toilet and retched into the bowl. Once he'd emptied the contents of his stomach, he splashed cold water over his face and hair and looked at his reflection in the mirror. Told himself he was going to get Pe back safe and sound if it was the last thing he did.

What now? he wondered. Then realized there was nothing he could do.

He hated having to be passive, wanted to be able to get out there and do something. Anything that would get him closer to finding Pe.

But all he could do was wait.

They'll call me, he told himself. They have to.

They wouldn't kill her.

Why should they murder a girl just because she was living with him, after all?

No, this was just meant to be a warning…

But it didn't make sense.

He told himself to stop thinking this way and start thinking like a cop. Told himself his time would be better spent on investigative work, rather than working himself up into a state. His mobile began to ring again. Maybe it was the kidnapper. He snatched it up. '*Diga?*'

'Luis, it's me,' said the familiar voice of his friend, Juan Gómez. 'I heard on the News that Pe's been gored. I'm so sorry… Where did the horn go in?'

'Just below the ribs, I think.'

'Was she conscious when they took her in the ambulance?'

'No.'

Silence.

'Below the ribs is the worse place to get it, right?'

'Not at all, Luis,' Gómez replied. 'Listen to me, it was Pe's choice to become a bullfighter and you've been against it all along, so stop beating yourself up… It's not your fault this has happened.'

'No, but I'm scared she won't pull through.'

'Of course she will.'

They both went quiet.

Gómez broke the silence: 'Going to have to learn to calm down a little, *hombre*,' he said. 'This sort of thing's going to happen from time to time, you know... practically an occupational hazard... Just going to have to live with it.'

'Guess you're right.' Velázquez wondered whether to tell him that Pe had been kidnapped, but then figured there was no point.

Silence.

'What are you doing now, Luis?'

'Sitting by the phone, waiting to hear.'

'Need to try to stay calm, *amigo*,' Gómez said. 'Do some of those deep breathing exercises I showed you—best thing to help you relax... Remember how to do it?'

'Sure... I'll try it now.'

'There anything I can do for either of you?'

'I'll tell you if there is.'

'You do that,' Gómez said. 'And try to take your mind off it—do something else... read, catch up on old stuff—anything so as long as you stay busy and stop brooding... And do remember to keep me posted, won't you?'

'Of course.'

They hung up, and Velázquez began to do the breathing exercises Gómez had talked about. He spent some twenty minutes on them. When he'd finished he remembered Anna Segura's manuscript sitting there on the bookshelf. He went over and picked it up.

... The man I had helped back to the safety of his family and comrades told everyone I had been fighting for the Republican army at Gandesa, and that I had saved his life when he was wounded. I explained that I had lost my papers in the fighting, which was easily accepted. Reinforcements had been sent to join the Nationalists, so the result of the battle was a foregone conclusion. Rather miraculously, then—or so it seemed to me—my conversion to the Republican cause was complete and quite free of complications. Just so long as I didn't come face to face with any Nationalists who knew me from my former life, I had nothing to fear...

Velazquez read on, about Pedro's life with his fellow

Republicans—*or maquis*, as they came to be called—in the mountains; of how he escaped into France in 1950 and didn't return to Spain until 1977, by which time it had become a democratic country—in name, at least...

Maybe he should never have come back, Velázquez found himself thinking. Because it seemed like someone could've been waiting to catch up with him.

His mobile began to vibrate.

CHAPTER 15

'Velázquez,' came the familiar voice of Comisario Alonso. 'We got another couple of bodies, in Calle Vidrio.'

One thought flashed through Velázquez's mind: *Please, God, don't let it be Pe...*

He said, 'The vics male or female?'

'Both male.'

Relief flooded through him.

Gajardo's old BMW was already at the crime scene, along with a patrol car, when Velazquez arrived.

The flat was on the top floor. There was no lift, and it was quite a way up. He had a fair amount of Scotch inside him, coupled with more grief and anxiety than he'd ever known, and was a little out of breath by the time he reached the top. The door to the flat was ajar. Velázquez took a moment to get his breathing under control, before he went in, calling out *'Hola?'* as he did so.

'In here, Boss,' Gajardo's familiar voice called back.

Velázquez walked to the end of the hallway and entered one of the bedrooms. Two bodies were lying on the bed. Both naked. Both male.

Both very dead.

There was blood all over the place: over the sheets, the carpet, the walls. The victims were both in their twenties. One got it in the side of the head, the other in the chest. The arm of one was draped over the chest of the other.

The one shot in the head was Ramón Ochoa. Velázquez didn't even know he'd been released from the Hospital de la Macarena. And hadn't Ochoa been under arrest while he was in there, and chained to the bed? None of it seemed to make any sense.

'They caught up with him in the end,' Velázquez said with a grimace as he turned to Gajardo. Then he saw the Judge, Cristobal Montero, and acknowledged him with a nod of the head.

Velazquez wanted to ask Gajardo what he knew—wanted to ask him how Ramón Ochoa could have ended up here. But he was loath to parade his ignorance in front of Judge Montero, who was as irritating, in Velázquez's view, as he was intelligent.

Cristobal Montero ran a chubby hand through his salt-and-pepper hair and let out a sigh. Dressed in a tailored grey suit with a silk white shirt and burgundy tie, he looked, Velázquez thought, like some modern-day Don Juan who'd come to Seville by way of Savile Row. His intelligent brown eyes fixed Velázquez with a thoughtful look. 'So what do you reckon, Inspector Jefe—are these murders connected to the others or not?'

Velázquez said, 'Right now all I can give you is an educated guess.'

'Which is...?'

'Very probably.'

'Different *modus operandi* from the one used on the two priests, though,' Cristobal Montero said. 'For my money we're looking at two killers, or maybe more... These killings, along with that of the Russian, Vorosky, could possibly fall into one category, and those of the priests into another.'

'Could be the same killer or killers using different methods to throw us off the scent, though, Judge.'

'Possible, I suppose, but I just don't see it.'

'We're only guessing at this stage, is the fact of the matter... We need to investigate these latest murders fully before we jump to any rash conclusions.'

'But time's the one thing we don't have, Inspector Jefe,' Judge Montero said. 'We need to act fast and put a stop to this spate of killings before things really get out of hand.'

Velázquez felt his head spin a little. He must be about a thousand times over the limit, and figured he probably smelt like the back end of a bender. A mint would come in handy.

Seeing Velázquez searching his pockets, the Judge brought out a packet of Marlboros and held it out. Velázquez declined with a little shake of the head. 'No, thanks. I quit years ago.' Cristobal Montero put the packet away.

Shouldn't be offering me a cigarette here anyway, Velázquez thought, this being a crime scene. Not that he was about to say this to the Judge: rank was rank, after all. But he was irritated by Montero's casual arrogance and ready-made theories.

He heard footsteps outside in the hallway and turned in time to see Gómez enter the room. Gómez gave Velázquez a friendly slap on the shoulder and said, 'City's getting to be like Chicago, huh?' then set to work.

Two *Científicos* entered and went about their work in a no-nonsense manner. One of them got down on his knees and started drawing yellow circles round the spots of blood on the carpet, while the other searched for fingerprints.

The Judge's brow constricted, so that a triangle appeared above the bridge of his nose. 'What are your thoughts, Inspector Jefe?'

'Contrary to what you were just saying, Judge, I think it's a fair bet that the same killer did for all of them, including Fathers Pedro and Aloysius.'

'What's the connection?'

'Name of the lad who was shot in the back of the head's Ramón Ochoa, Judge... he was being framed for murdering the two priests... Then whoever tried to frame him stole my car and used it to run him over, in an attempt to frame me for his murder... He was in a coma for a while, but he survived.'

'Not for very long, though, Inspector Jefe.'

'Unfortunately his luck ran out.'

'Okay, so assuming your theory's right, who was doing the framing, any ideas...?'

'Has all the signs of a turf war.'

'So you think all of the murders are linked, including that of the Russian?'

'I'd put this month's salary on it, if I were a betting man.'

'We're not running a betting shop here, Inspector Jefe, nor is the court. I can't build a case by basing my investigation on luck!'

'I'm well aware of that, Judge.' Velázquez had to work to conceal his irritation. 'We're working round the clock and doing everything we can. But we just need more time.'

Gajardo said, 'But these two guys are gay, Boss.'

'So…?'

'Hardly look like your typical pair of gangsters to me.'

'There you go thinking in stereotypes again, José.'

Velázquez turned to Gómez. 'What can you tell me about the time of death, Juan?'

'Temperature of the bodies tells me they were both killed sometime between eight and twelve hours ago… What's more, anal sex took place.'

'Regular Romeo and Juliet,' said Gajardo.

Gómez gave him a look that Velázquez understood only too well. Gajardo had his good qualities: he was honest and hardworking; but he could be bigoted and narrow-minded as all hell. Velázquez wondered how the man's wife, Almudena, ever put up with him. Then he remembered the stories Gajardo had been telling lately about his having to sleep on the sofa, or even in his car on occasion, and figured that she *wasn't* putting up with him.

Judge Montero said, 'Lucky it's me here tonight and not Ernesto Sanz Rivera.'

Gajardo gave him a questioning look.

'Slightest hint of homophobia and he'd have your balls in a sling.'

'Gay, is he?'

'No, but he hates bigots, sees them as a hangover from

the Franco era... that whole homophobic *Lord Of the Flies* mentality.'

'What...?'

'Title of a novel,' Velázquez hastened to explain. 'Group of bigger schoolboys hunting the smaller ones on a deserted island.' He knew this because Pe had read the book and told him about it.

'And do they catch them or what, Boss?'

'Cook one of them on a spit.'

Gajardo manfully volunteered to handle the prickly job of calling in on Señora Ochoa on his way home, to inform her of Ramón's death; Velázquez could hardly go himself, given the highly sensitive nature of his involvement. He was left instead with the job of speaking to the neighbours in the block.

He rang the bell to the flat next door, and had to wait a while before an old man in plaid dressing gown and slippers came and opened up. Velázquez showed the man his ID, apologized for waking him up. 'There's been a double murder next door,' he said.

The old man's mouth opened, revealing a couple of lonely yellow molars while his thick grey brows pointed to twenty to four.

'Just wondered if you heard anything, *señor*?'

'No... but when did it happen?'

'Can't be totally certain, but we think sometime between around three and seven p.m... Were you home at that time?'

The man nodded.

'But you didn't hear or see anything?'

'No, nothing at all.'

Velázquez thanked the man and apologized again for waking him.

'I only wish I could help,' the man said.

Velázquez spoke to all of the neighbours on the top floor, then to the people who lived on the floors below, but nobody had heard or seen a thing. Killer probably used a silencer, Velázquez thought, as he made his way back out to his car. The street was quiet as a stage set with no actors on it. Yet up there on the top floor of the building he'd just left, two young men had been murdered.

That's five have been killed now, he told himself.

And Pe had been taken.

Juan Gómez had said the place was becoming like Chicago. Something strange was going on for sure. Seville was normally one of the most peaceful of cities.

He started the engine up, buzzed the windows down and set off for home; but before he got there he decided he couldn't face the place without Pe. So he just drove around the streets.

He figured he must have drunk the best part of a bottle of Scotch earlier, and yet he felt more or less sober now, as the warm breeze blew in and tossed his hair about. All the shock and stress, he supposed. Had the effect of neutralizing the alcohol in your system.

His mobile began to vibrate in his pocket.

CHAPTER 16

'It's me, Luis,' came Gómez's voice.

'*Hola*, Juan… what's new?'

'We've got an ID for the other vic–name's Arturo Villanueva… his *carné* was in his trouser pocket.'

'Thanks for letting me know.'

'Catch you later.'

They hung up, and Velázquez continued to drive around the city's semi-deserted streets. Then his mobile began to ring again, and he grabbed it, certain that it was the kidnapper this time. But it turned out to be Gajardo. 'Thought you'd have gone home to bed by now, José,' Velázquez said.

'Don't feel like sleeping Boss… you know me, a workaholic if there ever was one.'

That's true, Velázquez thought. Nobody put more into the job than Gajardo, in terms of effort and commitment alone.

'Just wondering if the kidnapper'd called back?'

'No, not yet, José,' Velázquez said. 'I'll let you know when he does.'

'Wanted to ask you earlier, but couldn't with the Judge and everyone there.'

'Did you tell Pilar Ochoa about Ramón?'

'Yes… left her place a while ago.'

'Thanks for doing that, José… How did she take it?'

'Looked like she'd turned into a chilli, Boss… Said she was going to make sure you go to prison for his murder… Tried to tell her your car was stolen, and that whoever drove it at her son stole it with that purpose in mind–to frame you…'

'What did she have to say to that?'

'Told me I was lying… said she knew I was covering for you because you're my boss… what cops always do, she said.'

'Not a million miles from the truth in a number of cases I can think of.'

'With the woman for some while, trying to get her to see reason, but she was too upset to listen. You know she complained to Comisario Alonso, saying it was your car that drove at Ramón? Reason why the Comisario gave the order to take the cuffs off and let him go.'

'I wasn't even aware he'd been released from hospital.'

'Discharged himself—very much against the doctor's orders... Lad clearly had the constitution of a *toro*.'

'And about as much brains... Should've listened to the doctor.'

'Might still've been alive if he had.'

'He might,' Velázquez said. 'Then again, these people were determined to get to him, one way or another... It was only a matter of time.'

'Guess you're right.'

They went quiet for a moment, then Velázquez said, 'Juan Gómez just called.'

'What was that about?'

'Name Arturo Villanueva mean anything to you?'

'Don't think so... Why—should it?'

'He's the other vic that was lying on the bed with Ochoa.'

'Oh... —no, doesn't ring any bells.'

'Nor with me,' Velázquez said. 'Listen. I want you to have Serrano or Merino positioned in an unmarked car outside the Ochoas' family home first thing in the morning.' He glanced at his Swatch. It was coming up to 5.30 a.m. 'I want photographs of everyone who enters and leaves the property... and if you can put names to the faces, so much the better.' Velázquez was driving along the river; the baroque façade of the Maestranza flashed by. 'Where are you now, José?'

'In my car, Boss... accidentally woke Almudena up when I got into bed, and she read me the riot act... Couldn't stay in the flat with Almudena going at it full tilt like that.' Gajardo yawned. 'Besides, I've been worrying about Pe too much to sleep… Let's hope we can resolve this first thing tomorrow, then—or later today, I should say.'

'Fingers crossed.'

'Sure it wouldn't be better to get the sound men over to listen in on the conversation when the kidnapper gets back in touch?' Gajardo said. 'Never know, they might be able to trace the call.'

'No, I wanna do this my way… Remember what I said—no one's to know about it, okay? You're the only person I've told.' Actually, you're the second person, Velázquez thought. Diego Blanco was the other one. Practically bit his head off at the time; but the man didn't seem like he knew anything about it.

'Okay, Boss. I'll call you later… And let me know if anything happens, yeah?'

'Sure will. *Buenas noches.*'

Velázquez started to feel sick. He returned to his flat to take his shot of methadone. Then he began to pace up and down the living room, his head full of thoughts of Pe.

After a while the sun came up.

Then his mobile began to ring again.

Velázquez picked it up. '*Diga?*'

'I want the CD-Rom, Inspector Jefe.'

'You're saying it's a film you want?'

That's right… Vladimir Vorosky's CD-Rom.'

'But I don't have any CD-Rom,' Velázquez said. 'Are you Bill, the Black Lady's friend?' The man sure didn't sound like him, unless he was putting on a false accent.

'I am more than a little surprised by your attitude, Inspector Jefe. I had been under the impression you were in love with your girlfriend, and that you valued her life…'

'I do… I do… I'll do anything you want… but what's this about a CD-Rom…?'

No response.

Velázquez said, 'Listen to me… if I had this CD-Rom of

yours then I'd gladly give it to you in exchange for Pe. But I don't know anything about it.'

'Then that's just too bad, Inspector Jefe.'

'What do you mean by that?'

'I'm going to call you the same time tomorrow on this number... If you have not acquired the CD-Rom by then you will never see your girlfriend again.'

'Listen to me...'

But the man had already hung up.

Velázquez felt as though a fist had thrust itself into his belly and twisted his guts; he dashed to the bathroom and vomited into the sink. He retched again and again, until there was nothing left in his stomach. Finally he straightened up, and looked into the mirror, gripping the sides of the sink with his hands. His face was pale, unhealthy-looking, and he was weak in the knees. He splashed some water onto his face, went out into the kitchen, made himself a strong mug of coffee, then paced the flat, sipping his coffee as he did so, and trying to work out how he was going to find the CD-Rom.

Vladimir Vorosky's CD-Rom, the man had said.

Was that why Vorosky had been killed?—For a CD-Rom?

But what could be on it that was so important?

Velázquez felt the sick feeling rising up in him again, and told himself to get a grip. He was not going to be any use to Pe unless he could keep his emotions under control. But that was easier said than done.

What I could do with now, he thought, is some heroin: the proper stuff.

That would help him keep his emotions in check.

He pushed the thought out of his mind: don't give in, don't let them win.

The kidnapper had called on the stroke of nine. He'd said he would call again, the same time tomorrow.

I've got twenty-four hours to get this fucking CD-Rom, Velázquez thought, or Pe's going to die.

I've got to do something—and fast, he told himself.

But a large part of him was panicking; he had to find a needle in a haystack, only in this case the haystack was as big as Spain, bigger even perhaps, and he didn't have the first idea about where to start looking. Through all the fug and fear, a name suddenly crystallized in his mind: Ramón Ochoa. More and more, he seemed central to the case. It might be an idea to go and talk to Ramón's mother again. If Ramón was at the heart of all the mayhem somehow, Pilar might know something she hadn't told him, some vital piece of information that she herself might not even realize was important but which could, with any luck, help him find the CD-Rom. Velázquez realized that he was clutching at straws, but right now there was nothing else around for him to clutch at.

No sooner had she opened up and seen who it was than Pilar Ochoa tried to slam the door in Velázquez's face. He was too quick for her, though, and managed to get his foot in the jamb. 'What you don't seem to realize,' he said, 'is that I was batting for Ramón all along.'

Pilar Ochoa's eyes were brimming with venom. 'Ramón's innocent... first you set him up, then you tried to kill him, and when you found out he was in a coma you went back and finished the job.'

'No, you're wrong—it wasn't me—somebody stole my car and used it to run him over, as well as to frame me while they were at it... the same people who tried to frame Ramón for Father Pedro Mora's murder... Then when Ramón recovered, they went back and killed him. But it wasn't me, I swear. He knew that.'

Pilar Ochoa seemed to take a moment to think about this.

'All I want is to talk, Señora Ochoa. I'm a police detective, not a killer.'

Velázquez could see from the look in the woman's eyes that she wasn't sure whether or not to believe him. 'Okay,' he said,

'I'll tell you something that I haven't told anybody. The people who killed Ramón have kidnapped the woman I love. They say they want a certain CD-Rom that belonged to a Russian by the name of Vladimir Vorosky, and I'm to get it for them by nine o'clock tomorrow morning. If I fail to get it, I'll never see my girlfriend again… She is the woman of my heart. You've got to believe me.' There was a pause. His heartbeat counted out the seconds as Pilar wavered: one, two, three, four…

'Okay,' she relented, 'you'd better come in.'

Velázquez entered the flat and was assailed by the smell of mothballs and polish, as Pilar Ochoa led him along a narrow parquet hallway into the small living room, off to the right. There were a number of religious icons on the shelves, and paintings of Biblical scenes crowded the whitewashed walls. 'Take a seat,' she said, and pointed to one of the two easy chairs.

Velázquez told her he'd just as soon stand. He was in a race against the clock, and felt better when he was on his feet. The noises of the street washed in through the open window: a car going by, a man calling to a friend, a woman laughing.

'So what is it you want from me?' Pilar Ochoa brushed a few stray hairs out of her eyes.

'I'm trying to find the person or persons who killed Ramón and his friend… but to do that I'll need to ask you some questions first, and I'm going to need some honest answers.'

'Fire away.'

'I need to know if Ramón knew Father Pedro Mora, the priest that was killed.'

'No, he didn't know him, but he was quite friendly with the other one there,' she said. 'Young chap with brown hair, wears glasses.'

'Father Antonio, do you mean?'

'That's the one… Ramón was an addict, and he was trying to help him kick the habit, got him taking methadone instead…'

'So he was a good influence on your son, then, Father Antonio?'

'Far as I can make out, yes.'

'And they were quite friendly, you say?'

'Seemed to be.'

'Can you tell me anything about the other two priests who were killed?'

'No, I never heard Ramón talk about them.'

Velázquez thanked Pilar Ochoa for her time and went out. His mobile began to ring just as he was climbing into his car: it was Gajardo.

'Just wondering if the kidnapper called you back, Boss?'

'Called on the stroke of nine.'

'What did he want?'

'Vladimir Vorosky's CD-Rom.'

'Come again?'

'What I thought,' Velázquez said. 'Anyway, we've got twenty-four hours to find it... If I don't have it by nine a.m. tomorrow then I'll never see Pe again.'

'Where are you now, Boss?'

'I'm about to go over to Jesus del Gran Poder, to talk to Father Antonio again.'

'Know what they say about great minds,' Gajardo said.

'You mean you're there now?'

'Just parked outside and thought I'd call you to find out if anything's happened before going inside.'

'Wait for me, then,' Velázquez told him, 'and we'll talk to him together.'

CHAPTER 17

They found Father Antonio arranging some flowers up on the altar. '*Hola,* Father,' Velázquez said. 'We need to talk some more.'

The priest's thick brows rose in bushy curlicue. 'How can I help you?'

'I know that you're a big fan of marriage, Father.'

'I am indeed... but what's all this about?'

Velázquez said, 'The girl I want to marry's been kidnapped... Kidnapper says he will call again at nine tomorrow morning, and he wants me to have a certain object by that time... If I don't have it by then, he assures me I'll never see her again.'

'Oh no... but this is awful.'

Velázquez said, 'I haven't got much time.'

'No, of course... but I really don't see how I can help.' Then he gave the Inspector Jefe a sly look. 'Unless you mean that you'd like me to pray for her...?'

Velázquez said, 'You knew Ramón Ochoa rather well, Father, didn't you?'

Father Antonio's eyes flashed with alarm. 'What's all this about?'

'Why didn't you tell us that you knew him?'

'I'm sorry, but I don't follow.'

'Come on, Father, stop trying to pretend you don't know anything,' Velázquez said. 'Ramón's been murdered and I've just come from his mother's place. She told me that you'd befriended him, and were trying to help him kick his heroin habit.'

'That's right... But what's that got to do with anything?'

Velázquez wasn't sure yet, but he sensed there must be some kind of connection. 'Perhaps we should go somewhere we can talk in private?'

'Yes, of course.'

'After you, Father.'

Velázquez and Gajardo followed the priest off along the aisle, through to the sacristy, and on into the room they'd used during the Inspector Jefe's previous visit. Father Antonio sat the other side of the large desk. 'Please sit yourselves down, gentlemen.'

The officers parked themselves on the two upright chairs, and Father Antonio said, 'So you want to talk to me about Ramón Ochoa, is that it?'

Velázquez nodded. 'Ramón was involved in something big, and whatever it was he ended up paying for it with his life... And I think you know what it was, Father.'

The priest grimaced. 'I have to say I feel uncomfortable about this sort of thing,' he said. 'I don't like divulging things that have been said to me in confidence–even, when the conversations took place outside of the confessional.'

'Father, the clock is ticking.'

'Okay... Ramón told me that he'd burgled a flat... he was very concerned...'

'Go on...'

'Look, I really don't know if I ought to be telling you this...'

'For God's sake, Father—'

Father Antonio clenched his fist. 'Okay, I can tell you... but you're not to tell anyone else, understood?'

'Okay, but out with it...'

'Ramón told me he burgled a flat and found a dead man lying on the bed...the man had been shot in the head.'

'Was it the Russian, Vladimir Vorosky?'

'That's what he told me afterwards, yes.'

'Can I ask you why you didn't report this to the police, Father?'

'I'm telling you now, aren't I?'

'At the time, I mean... as soon as Ramón told you what happened?'

'Your people had already discovered the body by then, so there didn't seem to be any point,' Father Antonio said.

'Ramón would have been arrested for burglary and possibly for a homicide, too—one which he didn't commit... He confided in me, Inspector Jefe.' Father Antonio's chest heaved, and he puffed out his cheeks. 'Locking him up in prison was only going to harden a lad like that... I saw that much straightaway.'

'Since when has the clergy in this city seen fit to set itself up as judge and jury, Father?'

'It wasn't a question of that, Inspector Jefe... Ramón was basically a decent lad... I mean, I sensed he was at that stage still where he could go either way, you know?'

'That you might be able to save him from a life of crime, you mean?'

'Exactly.'

The two men looked at each other in silence. Velázquez mopped his brow with the back of his hand. 'Okay, so what else did Ramón tell you?'

'He found the briefcase and brought it away with him.'

'What did he do with it?'

'I was just getting to that,' Father Antonio said. 'I suppose he must've taken whatever money was in there... but he gave me a CD-Rom and asked me to keep it for him.'

Velázquez nearly jumped out of the chair. 'Have you watched it?'

Father Antonio shook his head. 'No.'

'What do you think's on it?'

'No idea.'

'Ramón didn't give you a clue?'

'No... he just seemed nervous about it.'

'Why do you think he chose you to look after it for him of all people?'

'I really don't know, Inspector Jefe... although I suppose a priest is probably the last person most people would come to if they were looking to... to...'

'Retrieve stolen property...?'

'Yes.'

Velázquez got to his feet. 'Where is this CD-Rom? Do you have it here or at home?'

'But what's all this about, anyway?'

'I really don't know at this stage… that's why I need to take a look at the CD-Rom.'

'But I gave it to the Russian…'

'What Russian would this be?'

'He came and asked for it.'

'And you just handed it over…?'

'What else was I supposed to do?' Father Antonio showed Velázquez the palms of his hands. 'It wasn't mine, after all.'

'No, precisely…'

'It belonged to the Russian it was stolen from, and he's dead.'

'It was stolen property, Father,' Velázquez said. 'And as such you should have given it to the police straightway.'

'But this man came calling saying that it was his and he wanted it back.'

'And you believed him?'

'The man said he'd let Vorosky borrow it.'

'So you gave him the CD-Rom?'

'Yes… did I do the wrong thing?'

'Dammit, Father…' Velázquez slammed the side of his fist down on the desk. 'I hope you realize I could arrest you for this?'

'On what charge?'

'Receiving stolen property, conspiring to conceal a serious crime… perhaps even conspiring to *commit* a serious crime…'

'But that's ridiculous.' Father Antonio's bushy brows worked through some tricky moves. 'I was merely returning what had been stolen to its rightful owner.'

'Yes, well right now, Father, the life of the woman I love is dependent on my retrieving it.' Velázquez had the feeling that he was dealing here with a man who was entirely cut off from the realities of the outside world. 'Had you ever seen this Russian before?'

Father Antonio shook his head. 'I'm sorry, but there's no way

I could have known this CD-Rom was so important to—'

'It's too late for that now, Father,' Velázquez cut him off. 'What did this man look like?'

'He was of average build and had short brown hair... spoke Spanish very badly—he was in his late twenties, and wearing jeans and a T-shirt...'

Velázquez reached into his jacket and brought out the photocopy of the portrait the artist had drawn, unfolded it and then held it up for Father Antonio to take a look at. 'This him?'

'Why, yes...'

Velázquez's mobile began to vibrate in his pocket.

'*Hola*, Inspector Jefe.'

'Who is this?'

'We haven't met before, Inspector Jefe.'

Man spoke with a strong foreign accent: possibly Russian, Velázquez thought. And said, 'What do you want?'

'I think we *both* want something, Inspector Jefe.'

Velázquez's heart was pounding like a herd of elephants running up a flight of creaky wooden stairs. 'Who are you?'

'It doesn't matter... I am nobody important.'

'I take it you were a friend of Vladimir Vorosky, am I right?'

'No, you are not correct, but that is not significant.'

'What do you want?'

'It is what we *both* want, Inspector Jefe...'

'Where are you?'

'I heard about your girlfriend...'

'I want to speak with her now.'

'You are misunderstand, Inspector Jefe. I am not the man who has take her.'

'Who, then...?'

'It is Mr. Big.'

'You're Russian, aren't you?'

'Yes, I am Russian, too... but it is another Russian... the one who he is running the *puticlub* in Camas.'

'How do you know this?'

'My girlfriend she work there.'

'At the *puticlub*...?'

'Yes. I go in and talk to her and she tell me about it. She hear one of them when they speak about your girlfriend on phone.'

'And you want to get your girlfriend out of there, right?'

'Correct... she don't want to work there, but they force her... The Russian he like her very much... She is very beautiful, you see... We are going out together when we both are living in Moscow. We are very much in love. We make our plans to be married, you understand... but then he take her, and he bring her over here to Spain with him. He put her in *puticlub* to work for him, and he make her do things with the men who go there. He make her do the things with him, too. That man he is an animal.'

'So you want your girlfriend back?'

'That's right... same as you, Inspector Jefe... So you see, we both want same thing.'

'Why doesn't your girlfriend leave the *puticlub*?'

'She cannot... he keep her there... She terrified of him and his people... They kill her if she try to escape.'

'I sympathize with you, but what do you want me to do?'

'That is very simple, Inspector Jefe. I want you to get my girlfriend from *puticlub* and bring her to me.'

'But that might not be very easy.'

'I do not say it will be.'

They both went quiet a moment, then Velázquez said, 'Okay, so that's what you want *me* to do... but what can *you* do for me...?'

'The answer to that question also is very simple, Inspector Jefe... You bring me my girlfriend, and I give you CD-Rom.'

'You mean that you have it?'

'But of course.'

'Where are you now?'

'That is not important.'

'I'd like to talk with you face to face.'

'So you can arrest me, you mean?'

Velázquez went quiet a moment. Then said, 'Okay, so bring me the CD-Rom, and then I'll go and get your girlfriend for you.'

'I am sure that would please you, Inspector Jefe... unfortunately it does not please me... You see, I am not fool... First you must get my girlfriend and bring her to me. And then I will give you CD-Rom.'

'What's on the CD-Rom?'

'I do not know.'

'You're lying.'

'No, I have not seen it.'

'But you must have some idea why it's so important to the man who has kidnapped my girlfriend?'

'I do not know, I tell you... I do not work for this man... I am not interested in his business... All I know is that he is very bad man, Inspector Jefe. Very, very bad... and he has my girlfriend. And she hear them saying things... things she should not hear but she hear, you understand? About CD-Rom and Vorosky and your girlfriend. She is in the bed with the bad man, and he think she sleep and he make a phone call, but she only pretend to sleep.'

'I see... well okay, I'll do what you ask. But how will I know which girl is the right one, when I go to the *puticlub*? And how will I manage to get her out, if people are watching her?'

'I can answer the first question. That is easy. My girlfriend's name is Lena. She is tall brunette. She have small tattoo of cherub on right shoulder. Her last name it is Buvrosky. I spell that for you.' The man did so, and Velázquez wrote it down. 'But you must not ask to see Lena Buvrosky when you go to *puticlub*. This very important. If you do that, they will know you go there from me. You must to ask for Rosa when you go there. That is name she have when she work.'

'Okay, and the answer to my second question...?'

'That is not so simple, Inspector Jefe... if I know how to liberate my girlfriend from *puticlub* myself then I would do it... But I am not policeman, and you are. This is a big difference.'

'Even so... a policeman can't just walk into one of those places and march out with one of the girls.'

'You must, Inspector Jefe, if you want the CD-Rom. It is the price I ask. My girlfriend for CD-Rom... you can do it, I think.'

They both went quiet a moment, then the man said, 'When you have CD-Rom you can give it to Russian mafia man to liberate your girlfriend, and everyone happy.'

'Except the Russian...'

'He will be happy when you give him CD-Rom.'

'Yes, but he won't be happy about losing your girlfriend, will he?'

'No, but I do not want for him to be happy about that... he's very bad man, I already told you.'

'Yes, but what I mean is, he will go after you.'

'We will go away very far where he can not find us.'

'Sounds like a good idea.'

The man said, 'You can say you are exchanging me my girlfriend for yours... a life for a life... That is fair, no...?'

'Yes,' Velázquez said. 'That's fair... But I need to get the CD-Rom as soon as possible, otherwise the kidnapper's going to kill my girlfriend.'

'I think you must move quickly, then, Inspector Jefe.'

Another idea occurred to Velázquez. 'Who is this Russian Mr. Big, anyway?'

'I see what you think, but it will not work, Inspector Jefe.'

'What...?'

'You can not get to him... the Russian he has always his guards—and they are special guards, trained and with guns. Nobody can get to him.'

'But who is he? What's his name?'

'We can to talk about this later, if you want, Inspector Jefe—after you bring me my girlfriend.'

The man was clearly no fool, Velázquez thought. 'Okay, so where do you want me to take your girlfriend, once I get her out of the *puticlub*?'

'I call you one hour from now and give directions.'

Just then, the church bells began to ring, and Velázquez noticed something strange: he could hear them ringing out of his mobile. *He's close by*, Velázquez thought, as the man hung up.

He dashed out of the room, and through the sacristy into the main part of the church, his eyes roving over the people who were praying. He saw a man go out through the main exit. Medium build, short brown hair, dressed in jeans and a T-shirt… as Father Antonio had described.

Velázquez dashed after the man, and caught up with him outside. 'Excuse me,' he said. 'Do I know you?'

The man turned round, and Velázquez took out his ID and held it up, quickly introducing himself as he did so. 'Could I see your *carné de identidad* a moment, please, *señor*?'

'What's all this about?' The man spoke with an accent that was as Andaluz as flamenco.

'I'm looking for somebody who meets your description, *señor*… Now, your *carné, por favor*…?'

The man took out his ID card. 'Here you are.'

Velázquez looked at it. The name on the *carné* was Enrique Sainz Romero. The man was clearly Spanish. 'For whom do you take me?' he asked. Velázquez handed the man his card and said, '*Gracias*.' Then he spotted another man at the other end of the square. The man appeared to be in a hurry. He was average build, short brown hair, wearing jeans and a T-shirt. 'Stop!' Velázquez shouted. '*Policía!*' The man turned to look back, then speeded up.

Subinspector Gajardo emerged from the church and called over to Velázquez who pointed and said, 'Stop him!' and sprinted after the man. Gajardo followed. The man hopped onto a motorbike, looking over his shoulder, his eyes masked by shades. 'You there, stop!' Velázquez shouted. '*Policía!*'

The man revved the engine and set off with a roar. Within seconds, he had reached the end of the narrow street, and Velázquez could only watch and curse as the motorbike turned the corner.

Gajardo drew level, shading his eyes as he looked up the street. 'Manage to get a look at his face, Boss?'

Velázquez shook his head. 'Too far away, and he was wearing shades.'

'So now what?'

'Man wants me to spring his girlfriend from the *puticlub* over in Camas.'

'Gathered that from listening to you on the phone.'

'Question is, how the *fuck* am I gonna do it?'

3

TERCIO DE MUERTE

The bull eyed the matador *with the cold stare of a killer—a killer that senses he is being outmanoeuvred, despite his vastly superior size and strength. And so there was a sense of caution and humiliation mixed in with his rage. Blood was running from the area in its neck, where the pics were lodged, as well as from his mouth. The bull was tired. Tired with the fight he'd be given. Tired of charging the cape over and over, only to find empty air behind it. The animal wanted to put an end to it. You could see it in his eyes. It would come any moment now: the moment of truth.*

The bull stamped once, twice, three times; then the matador *cried,* Toro! Toro!

CHAPTER 18

Half an hour later, Velázquez and Gajardo were sitting in Gajardo's car across the street from the Russians' *puticlub* out in Camas.

Velázquez turned to his number two. 'You stay in the car, José.'

'Sure you don't want me to go in there with you?'

Velázquez shook his head and said, 'If I'm not back out within twenty minutes then you'd better call the cavalry.' He got out, crossed the street, and went in through the front entrance of the club past the blond gorilla on the door, who just looked at him.

After the bright sun and intense heat of the street, the relative darkness of the small lobby was a shock to the senses. Velázquez passed through the wooden swing doors, into a large bar. There were a couple of girls dancing on poles on a stage in the middle of the place, and there were booths around the walls, most of which were empty. Little early in the day to be doing much business, the Inspector Jefe presumed. The clientele was made up of mostly seedy-looking guys in their forties or fifties, and the girls were young and could have just stepped out of *Penthouse* magazine. There must have been twenty-five people in the place, and seven or eight of them were girls. Mostly blondes, Velázquez noticed, although he spotted a brunette and a redhead. He doubted if any of them were Spanish. Certainly didn't look it. They would've been transported over here with lots of promises that were about as real as the fake boobs most of them had, Velázquez figured, as he made his way over to the counter.

He got the attention of the bull working the bar. Guy must have weighed in at a good 130 kilos, all of it solid muscle, and had a short brush of blond hair that you could have used to sweep the floor, if he hadn't been the sort to break your neck before you tried it. Velázquez ordered a San Miguel.

As the man bent down for a bottle, a girl appeared at Velázquez's side. She had the same short skirt, blonde hair and fake boobs as the rest of the girls in the place. Velázquez could tell her boobs were false because they looked harder than natural ones, for a start, and like they were further apart.

Arnie Schwarzenegger's twin set the San Miguel down on the counter before Velázquez, along with a glass. Velázquez paid him, conscious as he did so that the girl at his side had just put her hand on his arm. 'You look like my kind of man,' she purred.

The girl had blue eyes and two rows of perfect white teeth. Velázquez wondered how much the orthodontic work she'd had must be costing her, figured she'd no doubt have to repay it all with interest. There'd be reductions for liposuction. Dental debts and boob bills. Not to mention transport costs and whatever it cost to clothe and feed her; then there'd be the interest charges that accrued, and whatever the guys who were keeping her happened to feel like adding on the top. The way these guys generally operated, the debts the girls had to repay would turn out to be perpetual, *eternal*.

Velázquez looked into the girl's eyes, searching for signs of a real person in there, something that the girl's keepers hadn't beaten or terrified out her. She should be suffering like hell, he thought, and look scared or depressed, or even just sad; but she didn't. What she looked was *horny*. He wondered if the girl was drugged up, figured she had to be, poor kid. 'You wanna come upstairs with me, sailor?' she purred. 'I could float your dinghy...'

'I'm looking for Rosa.'

'What's the matter, don't you like me?' Her pout was a master class on false innocence. 'Ain't nothing Rosa can do for you that I can't do better, baby... Why don't you come upstairs and let me show you my map of India?'

'I want to see Rosa.'

The girl pointed along the bar to another blonde, who could have been her identical twin sister. The second girl looked over, saw the first girl gesturing and came to join them. 'Your friend's here,' the first girl said.

Velázquez smiled. 'You'd be Rosa, right?'

The second girl nodded. 'Hi, sugar... you been in here before?'

'No, but a friend of mine has and he recommended you, said you knew how to show a guy a great time.'

'Your friend sounds like an intelligent man.'

'Oh, he's that all right.'

'What's his name?'

'Juan Rodriguez,' Velázquez improvised.

'I think I know the man you mean.'

The first girl said, 'Enjoy,' and made herself scarce.

'We will,' Rosa said. Then she looked at Velázquez: 'You wanna buy me a drink first, or'd you prefer to go upstairs straightaway?'

'Upstairs sounds good.'

'Wait a moment,' Velázquez said, once they were inside the room. 'Don't undress, I need to talk to you.'

The girl shrugged. 'Sure, whatever you fancy... so long as you realize it'll cost you the same.'

Velázquez looked at her. 'Your boyfriend sent me.'

A look of fear came into the girl's brown eyes.

'He wants me to take you to him now.'

'You're crazy as a goat.'

'He says he loves you, and that you love him... is that right?'

The girl was looking at Velázquez, but he could tell she didn't really see him. She was travelling back in time, through clouds of whatever drug it was her keepers filled her with, to the clean happy days when she and the man she'd been going to marry were seeing each other in Russia.

'He says nothing's changed,' Velázquez said.

'Everything's changed.'

'Not for him... he says he still loves you like the first day he saw you.'

The girl seemed to snap out of her reverie. 'Do you know what they will do to us both if I leave here?'

'But he's going to take you somewhere far away... somewhere they'll never find you.'

Conflicting emotions seemed to be fighting it out inside the girl. 'It's too dangerous.'

'Don't be stupid, Lena... this is your only chance of ever living a normal happy life.'

'*Lena*,' she said. 'He told you my name.'

Velázquez nodded.

'That's my old name... the one I used to have before I came here. Now I am Rosa.'

'It's not your old name, Lena, it's your *real* name. There is no Rosa. She's a made-up person. She was created by the monsters who brought you to Spain and keep you imprisoned here.'

The girl looked at him as if she were trying to summon the courage to hope.

'My friend is waiting for us in a car outside,' Velázquez said. 'Now what's the quickest way out of this place?'

'Out through the bar, the way you came in,' she said. 'But everyone will see us... they will stop us.'

'No, Lena.'

'Yes, they will... One of the other girls tried to leave and they stopped her... then they beat her so badly afterwards she couldn't walk properly for a month.'

'Well, that's not going to happen this time.'

'Have you seen Sergei, the gorilla they have for a barman?' she said. 'And then there is Boris, who is not so strong but he is so violent even Sergei is scared of him... There are many others like them, and they are all armed. You are no match for them, believe me.'

'Perhaps I should tell you that I'm a police detective.' Velázquez took out his ID and showed it to her. 'They'll have to let us leave.'

'But they'll kill me and Fyodor once they catch us,' she said. 'I already told Fyodor this, when he came into the club to talk to me. I told him he should forget it and leave me.'

'They will never catch you, I promise,' Velázquez said, although there was no way he could be totally certain of this. 'You just need to be brave this one time, okay? Can you do that?'

The girl looked into Velázquez's eyes for what felt like ages, then she nodded.

'Are you ready to leave?'

'Yes… all right.'

'Come on, then. Hold my hand and don't let go, whatever happens, all right?'

They left the room, went back down the stairs, passed through the curtains, and crossed the long bar. Before they got to the swing doors, one of the bouncers came and blocked their path. Patchwork white and gold teeth, eyes that looked like they'd been rented from the reptile house at the zoo, the guy sure didn't *do* pretty. 'Where you think you're going?'

Velázquez said, 'I'm a police detective and I need to take this young lady for questioning.'

'She don't know nothin'.'

'I'll be the judge of that.'

'Questionin' about what?'

'I have reason to believe that one of her clients is involved in a case of serious fraud.' Velázquez took out his ID and held it up. 'Afraid I can't tell you any more than that at this moment in time.'

The man snatched Velázquez's ID from his hand and took a close look at it. 'She's workin'.'

'Yes, I realize that… I won't keep her long.'

The man handed Velázquez's ID back to him, and looked as though he were in two minds about whether to allow them to leave. 'This is very irregular,' he said. 'Girls are not allowed to leave when they workin'.'

'Can't be helped, I'm afraid… unless you'd like me to get the Vice Squad in here and shut the whole place down.'

'Hey, this place is legal.'

'Not sure my friends in the Vice Squad would agree, judging by some of your practices.'

'What practices…?'

'Sounds from the way you're talking that you keep the girls who work for you here incarcerated.'

'They free to come'n go as they please.'

'Really?'

'Yeah… you only gotta ask any of them.'

'In that case, you won't mind if I borrow Rosa for a few hours, then, will you?'

The man looked at the girl and said something in Russian; then he stood aside.

The sun hit them like a bolt of molten iron as they made their way across the street to where the car was parked. Velázquez opened the back door and helped Lena get in, before climbing in after her. You could have fried up a mixed grill on the back seat, but at least he'd got the girl out of there.

'What did that animal in there say to you in Russian, Lena?'

'He said I'd be food for the fishes in the sea if I'm not back by seven o'clock this evening.'

Gajardo put the car in gear and they set off through the sun-blanched streets. Minutes later they were crossing Triana bridge. Gajarda had to slow down for a horse and carriage with a smartly dressed family in it to pass in front of them. Velázquez looked out through the window, at the couples sitting under the broad parasols at the tables spaced out along Calle Betis on the riverbank. People who were dining out and enjoying each other's company. Velázquez found himself envying those people their freedom. How he would have liked to be with Pe now, sitting at one of those tables. 'Where are you taking me?' Lena asked him.

'That's up to your boyfriend.'

Minutes later, Velázquez's mobile started to ring. '*Diga?*'

'It's me, Inspector Jefe. Have you got Lena?'

'Yes.'

'Good man… let me speak to her.'

Velázquez handed the phone to Lena, and listened to her talk in Russian. As she spoke, tears ran down her cheeks, and she wiped them away with the back of her hand. Then she handed the phone back, and Velázquez asked the man where he wanted to meet up.

'I'm in farmhouse on road to Dos Hermanas,' the man said. 'I give you directions where to go, okay?'

The farmhouse was right out in the middle of nowhere. The outside walls had been painted white, the pitched roof was covered with red tiles, and the house looked like it must have two or three bedrooms. It was surrounded by fields that ran into hills in the distance: hardly the sort of place where an immigrant like Fyodor would be likely to find work easily. Maybe he'd brought enough money over from Russia to support himself while he was here, Velázquez thought, and so he didn't need to find a job. If he'd only come here with the idea of freeing Lena, then he wouldn't have been planning on staying here for long anyway.

A hot breeze blew up, bringing smells of the dry land with it; then, before they got to the front door of the house, it opened. On seeing her hero step out onto the doorstep, Lena rushed at him, and the pair hugged each other in a passionate embrace. The man—Velázquez heard Lena call him 'Fyodor'—didn't look like any Brad Pitt or Clark Gable to the Inspector Jefe, with his skinny frame and wild eyes, but Lena didn't seem to notice

153

or care too much, and the happy couple continued to celebrate their reunion by hugging and kissing, and uttering sweet nothings in Russian. Then they parted, and the man, Fyodor, looked at Velázquez and said, 'I am sorry, Inspector Jefe. You must please to excuse us. We are behaving like the children… but we are too happy.'

'I understand.'

Fyodor offered Velázquez his hand and they shook. 'I want to thank you for bring to me my Lena.'

Velázquez said, 'I just hope you're both very happy together.'

'Don't worry, we will be… but we must go somewhere far away from here, where we can be safe.'

'That sounds like a sensible idea, if I might say so.'

'And who is your friend?'

'Subinspector Gajardo, meet Fyodor.'

The two men nodded at each other.

'Please.' Fyodor threw out his arm. 'Come inside.'

'I have no time to waste,' Velázquez said. 'I've fulfilled my side of the bargain, and now it's time for you to fulfil yours… I need the CD-Rom.'

'Yes, of course… but please come inside and we can do business there.'

Fyodor turned and led them in through the door, into a small hallway, and then off into the main living room. There was a brick fireplace with a natural coal fire, and framed drawings and paintings of country scenes adorned the whitewashed walls. 'Please sit down,' Fyodor said.

'No, I've already told you I'm in a hurry… I want the CD-Rom.'

'And you will have it, Inspector Jefe.'

'I'm in no mood to be kept waiting around, Fyodor.'

'It is with my brother.'

'But that wasn't part of the deal.'

'I give to him for safe keeping.'

'Why on earth did you do that?'

'In case the people who was keeping Lena they catch me… I did not want to risk that they find CD-Rom.'

Velázquez's chest heaved as he worked to keep his temper under control. 'Listen to me, Fyodor. I went to the *puticlub* and got Lena out of there for you at some risk to both of us… because there was no saying how the goons that run that place might behave… But she's here. And you gave me your word you'd have the CD-Rom for me.'

'I do have it, Inspector Jefe… only not here. It is with my brother, Vassily.'

'So tell him to come here right now… My girlfriend will be killed if I don't have the CD-Rom when the kidnapper calls at nine o'clock tomorrow morning. Do you understand that?'

'Yes, and you will have it… There is nothing for you to be worry about, you really must believe me.'

'So get your brother here.'

'Vassily is in Tarifa… we must go to him, and he will give you CD-Rom.'

Velázquez took a deep breath, looked at his watch, started counting to ten. Got to five.

'There's plenty of time.' Fyodor smiled.

'Want me to come with you, Boss?' Gajardo asked.

'No, you drive back to Seville, José… you're going to have to take charge while I'm gone. And keep me updated, okay?'

'Will do, Boss. *Adios.*' Gajardo went out.

Fyodor said, 'We can take my Volkswagen.'

CHAPTER 19

The euphoria that had swept over Fyodor and Lena on finding themselves reunited had cooled into an edgy nervousness by the time they were on the road headed for Tarifa. They were talking in Russian, and Velázquez said it would make him feel a whole lot better if they spoke in Spanish from now on.

'Makes me wonder,' he said, 'if you're both up to something that you don't want me to know about.'

'All I just said,' Lena replied, 'is that the same car's been on our tail for the past twenty minutes.'

'Nobody is on our tail, *guapa*,' Fyodor sought to reassure her. 'Is just going to same direction we are. There only one road.'

Velázquez watched Fyodor as he peered in the mirror: the man's eyes were charged with about as much tension as jump leads, even if he didn't want to show it.

Lena said, 'Why don't you slow down, Fyodor, and let the man overtake?'

'Is no overtaking on this part of road.'

'Try it and see what he does.'

'Okay.'

So Fyodor slowed down, and it wasn't long before the driver in the car behind was flashing his lights at him; then the man took a chance and overtook, driving at sixty kph into a bend. 'Spanish drivers,' Fyodor laughed and shook his head. 'They sometimes not have many patience.'

It's true, Velázquez thought. We Spanish are not a patient people.

Minutes later, they passed Gibraltar, the Rock rearing up out of the water like a huge craggy molar that almost seemed close enough to touch. It was hard to believe that people actually lived out their lives on that shapeless and inhospitable-looking piece of stone. Lena said she'd always wanted to go there.

'We go one time, Lena,' Fyodor said. 'But not today.'

'No, we won't. We'll never go there now, and you know it.'

'Hey, we free to go where we please.'

'No, that's not true,' Lena said in a quiet voice.

'Hey, we just got you free from that place, Lena, and we together now... that is what is so important, huh?' Fyodor glanced in his mirror, as if to test the effect of his words on the woman he loved. 'We go there to Gib one day, *querida*, but not today, huh?'

'No, we'll never go there.'

Fyodor let out a sigh and shook his head.

They pressed on in silence, and it wasn't long before the road started to get more bendy than a sleeping python; and somehow Velázquez had a strange, creepy feeling, like they were heading towards the end of the earth. Or towards some lost stretch of land that the sea had spewed up long ago, but which civilization had yet to make its own.

'You not say much, Inspector Jefe,' Fyodor said.

'Your brother had better be there with the CD-Rom.'

'Of course... he wait there for us now.'

They continued in silence until they got to Tarifa.

The beach, which was a few miles further along the coast, drew surfers every summer on account of its high breakers, but the town itself turned out to be a strange, eerily empty sort of affair, full of echoes that ran along the ancient castle walls and the whisperings of the wind; and as for the port, Velázquez couldn't help feeling it was just the sort of place you'd expect some unremarkable-looking little tug to pull in carrying an illicit cargo sent over from Sicily or Afghanistan or Tangier—the latter, only being a short thirty-kilometre hop over the water.

They drove through the windy streets, past the old castle walls, and then they came to the cathedral and Fyodor told Velázquez to pull over. 'It's little pizza restaurant where Vassily say he is waiting for us—near to the cathedral, he say.'

They climbed out of the car, then walked round the back of the cathedral and saw a pizza restaurant up ahead. The warm wind, somehow full of echoes and secrets, was tossing Velázquez's hair about, and his heart was playing hopscotch in his chest as they walked up to the corner and entered the place.

It was a long, rectangular-shaped affair, and a large bear of a man was sitting alone at a table at the far end. A bear with a big head covered in short brown hair; the white face was broad and had a flattish, red, vodka-drinker's nose in the middle of it. The man got to his feet when he saw them, and looked very happy to see his brother. The two men hugged and kissed each other on the cheek.

'Look,' Velázquez said, 'I didn't come here for a social visit. Where's the CD-Rom?'

'I have it here.' Vassily reached inside his brown leather jacket.

Velázquez did likewise and brought out his gun. He held it low against Vassily's belly.

'Fyodor told me you are a policeman,' Vassily said.

'That's right, I am… Now sit at the table, nice and slowly, the three of you.'

They did as they were told, and Velázquez sat down with them, timing it so that he moved as they did. 'Right, now perhaps you ought to know that my gun is pointing at a part of your anatomy you probably value fairly highly, Vassily. You get my drift?'

Vassily nodded. 'But what's with the gun?'

'It's just what you might call a precaution… in case either of you get the silly idea into your head to try and trick me.'

'But I have the CD-Rom here.' Vassily held it up.

'You brought a laptop, like I said?'

'Yes—here.' Vassily pointed to a black case on the floor.

'I need to see it.'

'What… now?'

'That's right. *Now*… For all I know the CD-Rom you've got there could be blank… or else it could be a pirate copy of *Mary Poppins*.'

'Okay, no problem, Inspector Jefe. You can watch it now on my laptop.'

Fyodor said, 'Who she is, this Mary Poppins?'

Once he'd got back to Seville, Velázquez headed straight for *Blondes*. He parked, entered the club, and spotted Diego Blanco sitting on a stool at the bar holding court to a bevy of young women. It was all enough to make Velázquez want to puke, and he shat in the milk under his breath as he made his way over to the bar, near to where the gangster was sitting, got the attention of the barman and asked for a large Johnnie, neat. 'Black or red?'

'Black,' Diego Blanco called through the melee. 'And it's on me.'

Velázquez turned and said, 'See you've got company.'

The gangster shrugged. 'How's the business going with your girlfriend?'

The barman put Velázquez's drink down on the counter. The Inspector Jefe picked it up and knocked it back in one. 'There somewhere we can talk in private?'

'Sure.' Diego Blanco picked up his gin and tonic, slipped down off his stool and the sea of cleavages parted to allow him to pass. 'Come with me.'

Velázquez followed the gangster's squat form along the end of the bar and through a doorway, the man's ponytail swishing this way and that as he walked.

Like an enormous tadpole on the shoulders of a baby rhino, Velázquez thought.

'Take a seat.' Diego Blanco gestured with his hand.

Velázquez sat down on the hard-backed chair and took the CD-Rom from his breast pocket. 'You got a laptop handy?'

'What's this all about?' Diego Blanco parked his squat form in the black leather swivel chair the other side of the large mahogany desk.

'I need you to watch this with me.'

'What's on it?'

'It's the CD-Rom that Ramón Ochoa stole from the Russian, Vladimir Vorosky.'

'The Russian that was murdered, you mean?'

Velázquez nodded. 'Why did you order Ramón to steal it?'

'I didn't.'

'Come on, Diego, don't waste my time. If you want me to help you try and run the Russians out of town, then you're gonna have to scratch my back a little first...'

'I had Ramón watch Vladimir Vorosky.'

'Why?'

'Why do you think?' Diego Blanco said. 'I wanted to know what the man was up to.'

'Did you send Ramón to kill him?'

'No, not at all... why should I have wanted Vorosky dead?'

'You tell me, Diego.'

'No reason at all... Fact is, Vorosky approached me, said he wanted to split from his boss, Boris Kerensky.'

'He say why?'

'Just said Kerensky wanted too much for himself... man was a greedy fucker.'

'So Vorosky wanted what from you?'

'Man wanted to come in with me.'

'Did you trust him?'

'Think I got to the top of the shit-heap by trusting people so easy as that?' Diego Blanco said. 'You wanna run a city like Seville, you need the balls of a *toro,* sure, but you also need the eyes of a fox. I wanted to find out what he was up to first, before I even considered his offer.'

'And did you end up agreeing to welcome him in with you?'

'Why would I do that?'

'You knew that he was trying to break away from Kerensky.'

'I know he *told me* that... which is why I had Ramón watch

him.' The gangster took a sip of his drink.

'What decision did you come to in the end?'

'Didn't… he was killed before I had time to consider it.'

'You sent Ramón to burgle Vladimir Vorosky's place, didn't you?'

'Not exactly.'

'Good as told me so yourself, Diego.'

'I may have told Ramón the man was keeping some money there, but that's something different… '

'In a briefcase?'

'Possibly.'

'What about the CD-Rom?'

'What CD-Rom would this be?'

'This one here.' Velázquez held it up. 'You telling me you don't know anything about it?'

'Mind telling me what the fuck you're talking about?'

'Where's your computer?'

Diego Blanco opened one of the drawers in his desk and brought out a silver laptop, placed it on the desk and booted it up. 'I still don't get what it is you want from me?'

'The truth, Diego.'

'I've just told you everything there is to tell… I don't know anything about any CD-Rom.'

The two men fell silent as they looked at each other across the desk. 'Vorosky was already dead when Ramón broke into the house… He took a briefcase and found a lot of cash in it and the CD-Rom. He gave the CD-Rom to a friend, asked him to hold onto it for him.' Velázquez fed the CD-Rom in, then moved the laptop so they'd both be able to watch the footage. 'Perhaps I should warn you, Diego, it's not pretty viewing.'

He glanced at the gangster from time to time, as the film rolled, and saw from the man's expression that the CD-Rom wasn't his idea of entertainment.

'This is fucking sick,' Diego Blanco said.

'But why'd the Russian want it so badly is what I don't get?'

'Blackmail material's the only explanation I can think of.'

'But how can it be if you can't see the men's faces?'

'Don't you ever get to see them?'

Velázquez shook his head.

'In that case,' Diego Blanco said, 'I see what you mean... it's all a bit of a mystery.'

'I was hoping you might be able to help me.'

'How...?'

'That you might know something I don't, I mean...?'

'Sorry.' Diego Blanco sipped his gin and tonic. 'Solving mysteries isn't my line.'

'It's creating them, you mean?'

'Not need to get sarky... I thought you'd come here to ask for my help?'

'Obviously that was a stupid idea.'

Velázquez took the CD-Rom out and put it back in his pocket.

'So when's the Russian gonna call you?'

'Nine o'clock in the morning.'

'You give him the CD-Rom and he hands your girlfriend over, that it?'

'That's the deal, yeah.'

'Very strange business, if you ask me... Sorry I can't help you. Truly I am.'

Velázquez was feeling clammy and like he was going to be sick. He realized that he needed a fix. Then told himself he didn't *need* one, he just *wanted* one. Okay, he wanted one *badly*, then... but he could beat this. He had the methadone to keep him going, and he was going to kick his habit. I am, he told himself.

I am.

He got up, trying to conceal his nausea.

Diego Blanco looked at him. 'You don't look so good.'

Velázquez went out.

CHAPTER 20

Once he arrived at the *Jefatura*, Velázquez went in search of a tekkie, hoping and praying that there was one available. He got lucky and found Luz Zorilla, gave her the CD-Rom and had her run the footage on a large screen.

'Kid can't be any older than thirteen,' Luz said. 'Maybe a year or two younger.'

'Hard to tell without being able to see his face,' Velázquez replied. 'Can't see the faces of any of the men, the sick bastards.'

He sighed, blew out his cheeks. Then held up his hand: 'Stop it there.'

Luz pushed the *pause* button, and Velázquez went up close to the screen. 'That piece of sculpture,' he said, pointing to a figurine that stood alone on the mantelpiece. 'Hone in on it for me.'

Luz magnified the figurine, so that it took up most of the screen. Velázquez stood up close and scrutinized it. It was the only distinctive piece on view. All the other ornaments and pieces of furniture had been cleared away.

'What do you make of it, Luis?'

It was a black and white piece of a woman dancing. A gypsy, by the look of her, Velázquez thought. 'It's rather impressive.'

'Yeah,' Luz agreed. 'I like the way the sculptor worked the hair, like you can see the waves in it… And the way she's been caught in motion, too…'

'Looks real, doesn't it?'

Luz nodded, still looking at the image. 'I wonder if it's an original.'

'That's what I need to find out.'

Luz looked at him. 'You think it might give you a handle on where this took place, that it?'

Velázquez nodded. 'If I can trace the seller and find out who he sold it to.'

'Sounds like a bit of a long shot.'

'Right now long shots are all I've got,' Velázquez said. 'I mean, that figurine's the only distinctive feature in the film, so far.'

'Don't forget the strawberry mark one of the guys has on his ass.'

'No, I noticed that, Luz... but it's gonna be kinda difficult to go around Seville asking men to drop their trousers so you can take a look at their asses.'

Luz grinned. 'I don't really see you as the type, Luis.'

'Let's see the rest of the film.'

Luz set it rolling again, and Velázquez felt the potent cocktail of anger and disgust return as he watched.

When the film ended, he had Luz run off a copy so he could take it with him. 'I've got to go and do something important now,' he said. 'But I'll need four more copies of the CD-Rom, and some blow-ups of the figurine and the people in the film, okay?'

Luz nodded. 'Sure hope you catch those sickoes.'

Velázquez took out his mobile and called his number two. It took a while for Gajardo to pick up. '*Hola*, Boss... Jeez, what time is it?'

'Sorry about the hour, José... did I wake you?'

'Yeah... but don't worry about it.'

One thing about Gajardo, you could call him any hour of the day or night and he was ready to spring into action.

'You get the CD-Rom okay, Boss?'

'Just watched it.'

'Learn anything?'

'Not much, apart from the fact that there's a group of perverts in Seville raping little boys.'

'Nothing to suggest who they could be?'

'One of them's got a strawberry mark on his ass, and that's it.'

'No faces…?'

'No, they took care not to give themselves away like that,' Velázquez said. 'Although there is one more thing… a small figurine in the background on the footage, which, if it's an original, we might be able to trace.'

'What do you need me to do?'

'Come and get the copies of the CD-Rom and the blow-ups from Luz Cano.'

'What about you?'

'I'm heading home to wait for the call from the kidnapper.'

'Okay, I'll head over to the *Jefatura* now,' Gajardo said. 'What I don't get, though, is why the kidnapper should want this CD-Rom if there're no faces on it.'

'That's what I've been trying to work out, José.'

'You sure it's the right CD-Rom, Boss?'

'Right now I'm not sure of anything.'

'You still sure you don't want to get the sound guys over to your place, see if they can trace the call when it comes?'

'No, I wanna do this my way, José.'

'Okay, Boss… so call me as soon as you know anything, okay? *Hasta luego.*'

Velázquez told Luz Sub-inspector Gajardo was on his way over, then he left the building and drove home. It was coming up to half-past five when he got back to the flat. He was shaking all over, and he only just reached the bathroom in time to puke into the tub, but too late to avoid soiling his pants. Disgusted with himself, he undressed, cleaned up and dumped his soiled clothes into the washing machine, then set it to wash before fetching the baggie from its hiding place. He'd left a stock of needles there, too, and he took one, then went into the kitchen and heated the heroin, his heart beating with excitement now. I'm *dying* for it, he thought, still more disgusted with himself.

But this was going to be the last time. He would take it just this once, to help him through, so he could do what had to be done to get Pe back safe and sound, and then he'd never touch the stuff again.

He plunged the needle into the vein on the inside of his elbow, and groaned out of sheer pleasure and relief as a monster of a *toro* went charging through his veins... Minutes later he was taking a hot shower, and feeling just fine. Then, dried, he put on fresh clothes: a pair of faded, stonewashed jeans and a black T-shirt from the Corte Ingles—both purchases he'd bought on a shopping trip with Pe. He rubbed some gel into his hair, then combed it so that you could see the rail tracks. He stepped into his leather slippers: another purchase he'd made on a shopping trip with Pe. He was being upbeat. He wanted to look presentable for when he was reunited with Pe later. As he told himself he was sure to be. There were going to be no hitches or glitches, he told himself. No gremlins or hobgoblins. Everything was going to be just fine.

He had a shaky moment in front of the bathroom mirror, as he spread shaving foam over his face. What if things didn't go okay?

He found himself imagining what he would do if anything happened to Pe. Imagined himself waging a personal crusade against the Russians who'd taken her. He'd start by burning the *puticlub* down, then go after the Mr. Big personally. Get him on his own some place, and go to work on the bastard...

Velázquez realized that he was letting his imagination run away with him. He reminded himself of the importance of acting like a pro at all times. Even now, when the wires of his private and professional lives had crossed.

Especially now, he told himself, as he started in with the razor.

Stay upbeat and everything would be okay.

Once he'd finished shaving, he went into the kitchen and fixed himself a strong mug of coffee with toast. He poured olive oil on the toast and ate it at the kitchen table. He wasn't hungry, but he forced himself to eat. He was going to need to be sharp and wide awake for Pe today, and it was hard to be at your best on an empty stomach.

When he'd finished the toast, he went and sat on the sofa, next to the phone, and waited. Thoughts of Pe flooded his mind. He remembered a time early in their relationship when he'd been making love to Pe on the beach at night, and they'd just slipped into a nice rhythm when some bastard showed up and nicked her handbag. Velázquez went after the guy, brought him down with a crashing rugby tackle and retrieved the handbag; but Pe was annoyed when he handed it back to her. Confused, he asked her what was wrong. 'I was just about to *come*, you bastard!' she yelled. And then they'd both laughed their socks off.

That had been four years ago. But it felt like yesterday.

Velázquez realized that he was still as madly in love with Pe as ever…which was precisely why he'd been thinking of ending the relationship.

Pe didn't deserve to be kidnapped just because she was living with a cop.

If she'd been with another guy none of this would have happened to her.

He realized that his thoughts were becoming circular.

That was supposed to be a sign you were depressed.

Who *wouldn't* be depressed, in my situation? he thought.

My girlfriend's been kidnapped all because of me… *of course I'm fucking depressed! Joder!*

Which was perhaps another way of saying he was feeling sorry for himself.

Wait a moment, he thought. Pe's the victim here, not me.

She deserved better.

Better than me, Velázquez thought.

And to think I was forever complaining about her decision to become a professional bullfighter, he thought.

Who am I to tell a girl like Pe what she can or can't do?

The phone began to ring. Velázquez's thoughts stopped in their tracks, and he picked up. '*Diga?*'

'*Hola*, Inspector Jefe.' He recognized the kidnapper's voice. 'Have you got the CD-Rom?'

'Yes… but I want to speak to Pe before I hand it over.'

'She's okay, I promise you.'

'I want to find out for myself.'

'You're just going to have to trust me,' the Russian said. 'You bring the CD-Rom to my people. They pick you up in a helicopter and bring it to me. You got that?'

'Yes.'

'I look at the CD-Rom, check it is the one I need…and if everything is in order, you get to leave with your girlfriend.'

'Okay, but when do I get to see Pe?'

'All in good time, Inspector Jefe,' the man said. 'And remember—you come alone.'

'Okay.'

'We'll be watching you… so if there's anyone coming behind you, the deal's off and you can say goodbye to your girlfriend forever.'

'There won't be anybody with me.'

'I hope not, for the girl's sake, because she seems nice… Contrary to what you might think, Inspector Jefe, I am not some crazy sadistic murderer… I am a businessman. I do only what is necessary for my business to thrive. I do not like to make nice young women disappear. I can do it…—and I *will* do it, if I need to. But it doesn't need to come to that if you are sensible. Do we understand each other?'

'Yes.'

'Good, I am glad to hear that, Inspector Jefe.'

'So give me a time and a place.'

'You got a pen and paper handy?'

CHAPTER 21

Velázquez pulled up in a parking area several miles south of Bobadilla. Sat there and waited, wondering when the fuck the Russian was going to call. And hoping that Pe was all right.

But of course she is, he told himself.

The Russian wouldn't have harmed her.

Why should he? What would he gain from that?

Nothing.

Case of a simple exchange. I give the man what he wants, and he lets Pe go. End of story. No reason to worry about anything.

Velázquez was nervous as fuck even so.

Then he heard what sounded like the thunder of a helicopter. He looked out the window and saw what looked like a giant metallic insect in the distance and coming his way. His mobile began to vibrate on his thigh and he snatched it up. '*Diga?*'

'Get out of your car, Inspector Jefe.'

'Then what?'

'Just get out.'

Velázquez did as he was told.

'Now look up.'

'I can see a helicopter.'

'Good… it will land in the field near to you… Walk towards it.'

The line went dead, and Velázquez set off into the field in front of him. He could see that the helicopter was starting to come down. The grass looked like it was getting a blow dry from some super-powerful hair dryer.

Velázquez began to run as he saw the helicopter land. He saw two men get out and come towards him. They were wearing tracksuits and Nike trainers, balaclavas, shades. They could be anyone.

He stopped as he got to within four or five metres of them. One of the men had a gun and it was pointing at Velázquez. 'Give me CD-Rom,' the other man shouted.

'Where is Pe?' Velázquez yelled back. The noise from the helicopter was deafening.

'First the CD-Rom.'

'No, I want to see her... Where is she?'

'She okay. Nothing happen to her. You do not need to worry... You give me CD-Rom and I take it to my boss. He happy then he let girl go.'

Velázquez thought he'd been a fool to think he could handle this on his own. But now he'd come this far, he had no alternative but to do as the man said.

He reached inside his leather jacket and the man with the gun jerked it and shouted. 'Stop or I shoot!'

'The CD-Rom's in my pocket.'

'Wait.'

The man with the gun took a couple of steps closer to Velázquez, then jerked his head and the other man came over and frisked him. He reached inside Velázquez's jacket and brought out the CD-Rom. 'This it...?'

'That's it.' Velázquez's heart sank. He felt as though he had played this all wrong. He was handing over the CD-Rom in return for nothing. Rage welled up within him. 'Tell that boss of yours that if anything happens to Pe Naranjo,' he yelled, 'I'll chase him down and kill him.'

'You will hear from my boss. He will call you... But you have to be patient. You are not in a position to make threats.'

The Russians made their way back to the helicopter, the one that was armed walking backwards and keeping his gun pointed at Velázquez.

The two men climbed into the helicopter, then it took off and went up into the sky. Velázquez felt like he was standing in a wind tunnel: his clothes were blown back against his body, and his hair was going every which way. He couldn't ever remember feeling so bad. I've made a right mess of this, he thought. I shouldn't have tried to do it alone. If Pe is killed because of this...

He realized that he had learned nothing. I got the man's CD-Rom for him, and didn't make him give me anything in return, he told himself. I've behaved like a fool. Like a fucking *amateur. Joder!*

Making his way back to his car, he cursed himself for allowing his emotions and fears to cloud his judgement. Need to get a grip, man, he told himself as he climbed in behind the wheel. No sooner had he started the engine up than his mobile began to vibrate in his pocket. '*Diga?*'

'It's me, Boss... Just wondering what's going on at your end?'

Velázquez said, 'I think I've probably acted like an idiot, José,' and told the Sub-inspector what had happened.

'Maybe you shouldn't've done it alone, Boss.'

'That's the very last thing I want to hear right now, the way I'm feeling.'

'Sorry, I didn't mean to...' Gajardo broke off. 'Anyway, the Russian might keep his side of the bargain now and let Pe go.'

'But what if he doesn't...?'

The two men listened to each other breathing down the line. Gajardo said, 'So now what...?'

'I've just got to hope the Russian calls me back.'

'I've got the copies from Luz.'

'Lock the CD-Roms in your desk and see if you can find out anything about the figurine in the blow-ups,' Velázquez said. 'We need to know who the sculptor is that made it, or who sold it... Anything you can come up with.'

'I'll go round some of the galleries and antique shops in the city, and see what I can find out. Shall I get Serrano, Pérez and Merino on it, too?'

'The less they know about this the better, José. Handle it yourself. And let me know straightaway if you turn anything up.'

Velázquez hung up and tossed his mobile onto the vacant passenger seat, then started the engine up and set off for Seville. He had just reached the outskirts of the city when his mobile began to ring. He snatched it up. *'Diga?'*

'It's not the right CD-Rom, Inspector Jefe.'

Velázquez swerved to miss a car, then slowed to a halt for a red light. His heart was busy doing somersaults. 'The fuck are you talking about?'

'The CD-Rom… you brought me the wrong one.'

'But it's the one that Fyodor's brother, Vassily, gave me…'

'Fyodor…? Vassily…? Who are these people?'

The motorist in the car behind was parping his horn. The light had changed. Velázquez set off again, steering with his right hand, jamming the phone to his ear with his left. Adrenaline raced through his veins like a wild bull. 'You know, the girl Lena's boyfriend…'

'Lena, yes, you took her… Where is she?'

'She didn't want to work for you.'

'She owes me money.'

'She seemed to think she'd paid you off.'

'Your attitude is most surprising, Inspector Jefe,' the Russian said. 'You are not talking like a man who loves his girlfriend.'

'Let me talk to her.'

'The CD-Rom, Inspector Jefe… I need the right one.'

'It's the one that Ramón Ochoa took from Vladimir Vorosky.'

'Who told you that?'

'I can't tell you that… but I know that my source is honest.'

'There were two CD-Roms, Inspector Jefe, and you gave me the wrong one.'

Velázquez hit the brakes as a pedestrian stepped out into his path on a crossing.

'Look, I need to speak to my girlfriend…'

The kidnapper had already hung up.

Tears streamed down Velázquez's cheeks as he headed along the Paseo de Cristobal Colon. He dried his face with the back of his hand, told himself he'd really fucked up this time.

Now what? he wondered, as he crossed the Guadalquivir.

He went up Blas Infante, turned up a side street and pulled over, reached into his jacket pocket and brought out the baggie he'd brought with him. There was still some heroin left in it: enough for a couple more hits, at least. And he'd brought a needle and a teaspoon, too. 'I think of everything,' he said aloud. Everything except for what I should be thinking about. He took out his lighter to heat the heroin in the teaspoon.

His mobile began to jive across the passenger seat as he jabbed the needle in, and he snatched it up. 'José?'

'You talked to the Russian again, Boss?'

'Just now,' Velázquez said, his mind reeling as the heroin exploded in his veins. He took a deep breath as he threw his head back on the rest, his eyes rolling.

He heard Gajardo say, 'Boss…?' down the line.

Velázquez swallowed hard, then said, 'Man says there are two CD-Roms and I gave him the wrong one, so he's keeping Pe until I bring him the one he wants.'

'*Mierda!*'

'How's your search for the sculptor going?'

'Got a name and address.'

'Spoken to him yet?'

'On my way to his studio on Calle Gerona right now.'

'What's the number?'

Gajardo told him.

'See you there in a few minutes.'

Velázquez saw Gajardo standing by his car up ahead; he pulled over and parked with two wheels on the pavement, jumped out and ran over to the door. The Sub-inspector pressed the buzzer to the studio, and a gruff masculine voice said, '*Hola*?'

Gajardo told the man who they were. 'We need to talk to the sculptor Antonio Ferrer.'

'That's me... What do you want to talk to me about?'

'If you come down, *señor*, then we can tell you...'

A couple of minutes later, the large wooden door creaked open, and they found themselves looking at a big man with a bushy black beard, dressed in a pair of baggy old jeans and a white T-shirt that did nothing to hide his beer belly. Gajardo took out the blow-up he'd brought with him. 'We need to know if this figurine is your work?'

Antonio Ferrer took the blow-up and looked at it. 'Yes, it is.'

'You are quite sure?'

'No question about it.'

'How many copies did you run off?'

'None... I'm an artist, not a factory.'

'Who did you sell it to?'

'Jorge Villalba, the politician.'

Velázquez said, 'You know where he has the figurine?'

The sculptor shrugged. 'In his home, I presume.'

'Have you ever been there?'

'Yes... once.'

'And did he have the figurine there?'

The sculptor nodded.

Velázquez took out notebook and pen, saying, 'Where does the man live?'

Antonio Ferrer took out his mobile and pushed a few keys. 'Here it is,' he said, and read out the address. 'But what's all this about?'

'Nothing important, *señor*,' Gajardo said. 'Just routine.'

The sculptor's dark eyes narrowed. 'Doesn't sound like it to me.'

'Thanks for your help, *señor* Ferrer.'

Velázquez turned to Gajardo, 'We'll take my car.'

Jorge Villalba's house was one of the beautiful old palaces on Calle San Vicente that were once the preserve of the Spanish aristocracy. Velázquez rang the buzzer but nobody answered. 'We need to get in there and take a look around,' he said.

'We'll need a warrant, Boss.'

'No time for that.' Velázquez pushed the buzzer again. There was no answer, so he pushed the buzzer to the flat below. A man replied, and Velázquez explained who they were. 'We've come here to speak to *señor* Villalba.'

The man buzzed them in, and they took the lift up to the top floor and rang the bell to the flat. Nobody came to the door, so Velázquez took out the lock picks he always carried with him and set to work. It didn't take him long to get the door open, and they entered the flat and started to go through the place. They started checking through the spacious and elegantly furnished rooms one by one, on the lookout for the small figurine... and found it sitting on the mantelpiece in the main living room.

They found something else there, too: a man lying on the sofa.

At first Velázquez wondered if the man was sleeping.

Then he saw the bullet wounds to the head and chest. The man was taking the long *siesta* from which there's no return.

Gajardo said, 'Seems we got here too late, Boss.'

Velázquez touched the victim's cheek. 'Not by long,' he said. 'Body's still warm.'

They checked the rest of the house, to make sure the killer wasn't hiding anywhere. But the place was empty.

'D'you reckon Villalba's one of the men on the CD-Rom, Boss?'

'Gotta be a good bet,' Velázquez said. 'Let's go and take another look at him.'

Gajardo followed the Inspector Jefe back into the living room. 'What are we looking for, Boss?'

Velázquez undid the belt on the victim's trousers, then turned the body over and slid the trousers down. 'Now there's a coincidence, José.'

There was a large strawberry mark on the victim's right buttock.

'It's the guy in the CD-Rom, Boss,' Gajardo said. 'They must've filmed it here... But who d'you reckon killed him?'

'You know as much as I do.'

'Just wondered if you had a hunch, Boss?'

'I'm a police detective, José, not Sherlock fucking Holmes.'

'I've known you to get hunches from time to time, even so.'

Velázquez took a chew on his lower lip. 'There's all sorts of possible lines of enquiry,' he said. 'There's the paedophile connection, for one thing...'

'That could apply to lots of people—I mean, most people hate them, right?'

'Yes, but here we're talking someone who hates them enough to commit murder.'

Sub-inspector Gajardo nodded. 'What are the alternatives you have in mind?'

'The victim's a politician, José...'

'And everyone hates them, too, right?'

'Maybe not as much as paedophiles, but you don't need me to tell you how much corruption there is in our political life.'

Velázquez took out his mobile and called the *Jefatura*. Stood there trying to work out what his next move should be as he listened to the ringtone. Then when the desk sergeant picked up, Velázquez identified himself and said, 'There's been a murder... I need you to get the Policía Científica team over here a.s.a.p.'

'What's the address?'

Velázquez told him, then hung up and said, 'I'm going to have another word with Father Antonio, over at Jesus del Gran Poder.' The priest had been holding out on him, and Velázquez was all out of patience.

'Want me to go with you, Boss?'

'No... I need you here for when the forensics and the fingerprint guys show.'

'Call me if you manage to turn anything up, okay?'

Velázquez drove the short distance over to the Plaza de San Lorenzo. Pulled up on the pavement outside the Iglesia de Jesus del Gran Poder, jumped out of the car and ran over the square, then went in through the Gothic archway and into the sacristy.

There was no sign of Father Antonio, or anyone else. Just as well, Velázquez thought. He was up to his nuts with trying to get the man to talk. Besides, he had a hunch Father Antonio might have put the CD-Rom in his office. Where else would a priest keep something like that? It had to be there or in the man's flat.

Velázquez tried the door and it opened. He rushed over to the desk and rifled the drawers. No good. What about the bookcase? He got down on his haunches and started taking the Bibles and prayer books out. Concealed behind them was a CD-Rom. He felt sure it must be the one he needed.

Velázquez put it in his pocket, then hurried back out to his car, climbed in behind the wheel and set off for the *Jefatura*.

CHAPTER 22

Velázquez found Luz Cano working at her desk. 'I've got another favour to ask of you, Luz.' Velázquez brought out the CD-Rom. 'This is a different one,' he said. 'I need you to do the same with this one as you did with the other.'

'Make copies?'

Velázquez nodded. 'First I need to watch it though, just like last time …and I'll probably need you to make some blow-up stills as well, okay?'

'Sure.' Luz took the CD-Rom, slid it into the laptop, then pushed *play*.

But this time nothing happened.

She tried it again.

No go.

'What's up?' Velázquez asked her.

'Must be encrypted.'

'Are you saying you can't play it without tapping in some secret code first?'

'That's right… I take it you don't know the code?'

Velázquez shook his head. 'There any way round this?'

'Only way's to break the code.'

'Which ain't gonna be easy, right?'

'It's a job for the experts.'

'*Joder!*' Velázquez had to work to get his thoughts and emotions under control. 'I'll need to have the best people working on it,' he said. 'If our people can't do it then get Spanish Intelligence involved—whatever it takes. And I need this done fast. It's an emergency and the clock's ticking.' He made to leave, then stopped at the door and turned. 'Oh, and I'll need you to make two copies for me to take a.s.a.p., like you did with the other one… and run off others for whoever you get working on it.'

'Okay, leave it with me.'

The Inspector Jefe drove back over to the crime scene, where Sub-inspector Gajardo was watching the Policía Científica team go about their work. '*Hola*, Boss,' the Sub-inspector said. 'Manage to turn anything up?'

Velázquez told him how he'd found the second CD-Rom but was unable to watch it because it was encrypted. 'What's been happening here?'

Gajardo shrugged. 'Nobody's telling me anything yet.'

'Still early days,' Velázquez said. 'I want you to come with me over to the Russians' *puticlub*.'

'What's the plan, Boss?'

'I'm going to leave a message for the kidnappers.'

It was dark inside the club when they got there, and cool on account of the air conditioning; it could have been anywhere, any time. A girl was busy trying to wrap herself around a metal pole on the stage. Her aerobic efforts were in marked contrast to those of the seedy-looking characters lined up along the bar: middle-aged Spanish males with thinning hair and thickening waistlines, nursing drinks and a vague desire to be young again.

Velázquez squeezed in between a couple of them, and told the muscled barman he wanted to speak to his boss. The Russian squinted, wary as a fox, then said, 'He's not here. What do you want?'

'Tell him I've got his CD-Rom, and I'm willing to hand it over in exchange for my girlfriend. You got that?'

The barman nodded.

'He's got the number of my mobile.'

'Okay.'

Velázquez turned and went back out, with Sub-inspector Gajardo in tow.

'Now what, Boss…?'

'We wait for him to call.'

'What if he doesn't?'

'Oh, he'll call all right.'

'What makes you so sure?'

'He wants the CD-Rom.'

Velázquez put the car in gear and set off.

'Where are we going, Boss?'

'May as well go and see how they're progressing with the code while we're waiting.'

The breeze that swept in through the open windows was hot as a hair-dryer as they drove to the *Jefatura*. Velázquez left the Alfa Romeo in the basement car park, then he and Gajardo took the lift up and went in search of Luz Cano, and they found her at her desk. 'Got our guys and Spanish Intelligence working on it,' she said. 'No luck as yet, though, I'm afraid.'

Velázquez's mobile began to buzz in his pocket. '*Diga*?'

'*Hola*, Inspector Jefe. I hear you have something for me?'

'I've got the CD-Rom.'

'You are sure it is the right one this time?'

'Yes.'

'How did you come by it?'

'How did you kidnap Pe?'

'Do you always answer a question with another question?'

'Only when my girlfriend's been kidnapped.'

'I see you have not lost your sense of humour, Inspector Jefe,' the Russian replied. 'We took her in an ambulance—but you already know this… Now answer my question: have you watched the CD-Rom?'

'No.' Velázquez was confused. 'But there's no way you could've known Pe was going to get gored during the *corrida*.'

'We took the precaution of drugging her beforehand… That way she was bound to lose consciousness before too much time had passed, and we had our men and the ambulance on standby, ready to take her when she did.'

'She was badly gored... for all I know you could be lying,' Velázquez said, 'and she could be dead, you son of the great whore!'

'Bullfighting is a very risky business, Inspector Jefe, it's true,' the kidnapper replied, 'but in this instance your girlfriend was not gored.'

'That's a lie—I saw the blood myself.'

'Not hers.'

'Huh...?'

'Our people had a bag of blood on hand, so as to make it *look* as though she'd been gored... Just a matter of having our man pour it over her tunic.'

'But how did you drug her?'

'There was something put in her energy drink she always has in the dressing room before a bullfight,' the Russian said. 'We are professionals and do our homework, Inspector Jefe.'

'But she could've been killed if she'd been groggy or passed out when the bull charged!'

'We doped the bull a little beforehand—not enough to make it too obvious, but just enough to slow it down and make it a little less aggressive... And we had a marksman on hand who would've been able to shoot the bull with a tranquilizer if it had been necessary, as well as a surgeon in the unlikely event there was an accident. The risk of something bad happening to your girlfriend was minimal, I assure you... And now I must tell you that I am getting tired of all your questions, and I need you to answer mine. Tell me, how can you be sure it's the right CD-Rom?'

'This one's encrypted.'

'I see... in that case, I would like to see it.'

'Listen,' Velázquez said. 'This time we're going to do things differently. I'm only prepared to make a direct exchange: the CD-Rom for Pe Naranjo.'

'For all I know this could be a trick.'

'This CD-Rom is from the same person, only difference being that this one is encrypted. I suspect that you can see the faces of the men on this one...which I presume is what you want it for... is it?'

'So you watched the other one, Inspector Jefe...?'

'I'm afraid I did... made me want to throw up.'

'Yes, there are some sick people out there.'

'Anyway, I'd say we have business to do.'

'Indeed.'

'This time we meet face to face... you bring Pe Naranjo to me, and I give you the CD-Rom.'

'I will need to check the CD-Rom is the one I want.'

'So bring a laptop.'

The line went quiet while the Russian gave the matter some consideration. Finally he said, 'You make a lot of demands for somebody in your position.'

'I disagree.'

'You talk tough, but I don't think you quite realize who you are dealing with.'

'I can play tough, too... Up until now I've been playing by the rules, but if anything happens to Pe Naranjo then the rulebook goes out of the window.'

'What do you mean by that?'

'Take that club of yours... something nasty could happen to it.'

'Such as?'

'I don't know... a fire, perhaps.'

'I hope you are not trying to threaten me, Inspector Jefe.'

'I'm simply telling you the way it is,' Velázquez said.

'You have a way of talking more like a criminal than a police detective.'

'I'm talking like a man who is prepared to do whatever it takes to get his girlfriend back.'

They both went quiet for a moment, then Velázquez broke the silence: 'Okay, let's try another way of looking at it... My girlfriend's life is nothing to you, correct?'

'She is my insurance.'

'You want the CD-Rom, I know... and I have it. So you bring your laptop and Pe Naranjo to some place where we meet. I'm sure you know the code to open the CD-Rom.'

'What makes you so certain of that?'

'The way I have it figured, you must've had one of your men plant the camera in the room at Villalba's beforehand,' Velázquez said. 'Must've been one of these tiny spy cameras that are easy to conceal. Am I right?'

'Go on.'

'So as I was saying, you can check the CD-Rom in the café where we arrange to meet. And then, once you've satisfied yourself that it's the right one, as I'm sure you will, I leave with Pe... That way we both win.'

'Okay, have it your way, Inspector Jefe... but you must allow me to decide where to meet, and you must come alone.'

'No—I'll be bringing my number two with me, and you bring one of your men with you... just the one, otherwise it's no deal.'

They both went quiet, and Velázquez listened to the Russian breathing down the line.

'Okay, Inspector Jefe,' the man finally broke the silence. 'You bring your partner with you, but I decide the time and place... I'll call you again shortly.'

The line went dead.

Velázquez reached into his jacket pocket, and brought out his baggie. Yeah, there was enough for another hit, maybe two, if he rationed himself... He told himself that he shouldn't do it, but knew this was one contest his conscience didn't stand a chance of winning.

Just until I've got Pe back, he told himself, and then I'll kick it.

CHAPTER 23

Just over an hour later, Velázquez was waiting outside of a café on Calle Juan de Mariano. It was a nondescript little affair. Not the sort of place where you'd ever expect anything exciting to happen…

Velázquez was nervous and fidgety. He kept looking at his watch.

A top-of-the-range BMW pulled up, and Velázquez's pulse switched to taurine mode. He exchanged glances with Gajardo; both of them were ready.

Two men climbed out of the car. One was tall and of medium build, dressed in a smart grey suit and carrying a laptop. The second man was short and stocky, wearing jeans, Nikes and black sports jacket. They came over to Velázquez and Gajardo, and stopped just in front of them on the pavement. 'Nice day for it,' said the one in grey.

'Usually is in Seville,' the Inspector Jefe said. 'But I thought it was only the English who like to talk about the weather.'

'Always been a big admirer of the English.'

'Not many of them here, except for the odd language teacher.'

The Russian's face creased in a forced smile. 'To business, then… Have you got the CD-Rom, Inspector Jefe?'

'Where's Pe?'

'In the car.'

'Get her out here.'

'First I need to see the CD-Rom.'

'No, either you bring her out here now or the deal's off.'

The Russian looked at Velázquez and didn't say anything.

'You can leave your friend here outside the café with Pe and Sub-inspector Gajardo,' the Inspector Jefe said. 'You and I can

go into the café and conduct our business at a table in there…
You check the CD-Rom out, then once you've satisfied yourself
it's the one you want, you take the CD-Rom and leave with
your friend and Pe stays with us. That way everyone's happy. It's
what we agreed.'

The Russian kept staring at Velázquez.

Velázquez stared back at him.

Seconds passed.

Finally the Russian said, 'And what are you gonna do if I say
no…?'

'I've already told you that.'

'I'd like to hear you tell me to my face.'

'I'll do whatever I have to, to bring you down… whether it's
inside or outside of the law.'

'I could have you shot, if you want to play it like that…
Don't go thinking that wouldn't be easy.'

'I'll take my chances.' Velázquez shrugged. 'But that cuts
both ways, of course.'

The Russian grinned. 'Okay, have it your way.' He nodded to
the man he'd brought with him, and the man went over to the
car.

Velázquez watched him open the door and help Pe out. She
looked over at Velázquez. If she was scared then she certainly
didn't show it. That girl hasn't half got some *cojones*, Velázquez
thought, his pulse turning up the volume a notch as he watched
the man take Pe by the arm and bring her over to the pavement.

Velázquez smiled at her. 'Are you all right, Pe?'

She nodded.

What a girl, he thought. Acting like this whole business of
being kidnapped were a minor detail. 'And now you're fighting
fit, huh?'

'Just about.'

'Okay, Inspector Jefe,' said the Russian in the suit, 'how
about we go and see to our little business matter…?'

'After you.'

Velázquez followed the Russian into the café. The place had a tiled floor, and there were pictures of bullfighters on the whitewashed walls. Several men were sitting or standing at the long bar. There must have been twelve or fourteen people in the place. Velázquez and the Russian went over to one of the vacant tables next to the window. 'You sit this side.' The Russian pointed. 'And put your hands flat on the table where I can see them.'

Velázquez did as the Russian said, then the man sat on the other side of the table. He took out his laptop and booted it up. 'The CD-Rom, Inspector Jefe.'

Velázquez took out one of the two copies he'd picked up from Luz earlier and handed it to him.

A young waitress came over and asked what she could get them. Velázquez ordered two coffees, just to get rid of her.

The waitress smiled and went away.

Meanwhile, the Russian had fed the CD-Rom into the laptop, and was now busily tapping away at the keys.

Velázquez figured the man didn't want him to see what was on it. He'd be able to see for himself, anyway, just as soon as the experts had cracked the code.

The waitress returned with the coffees, then went away again.

The Russian had stopped tapping at the keys by now. He must have got the CD-Rom open, Velázquez thought. And said, 'It's the right one this time, isn't it...?'

'One moment, Inspector Jefe... I would like to see a little more.'

Velázquez glanced at his Swatch. The second hand was dragging like a bastard. He glanced through the window and saw Gajardo and Pe standing out there, along with the other Russian. Rivers of sweat were coursing down Velázquez's back.

The Russian turned the computer off, then closed the lid. 'This time you have delivered the right CD-Rom, Inspector Jefe,' he said. 'Congratulations on an excellent piece of work... now you are free to take the girl.'

Velázquez got up and left the café, with the Russian close

behind him. When they got outside, Velázquez reached into his jacket for his gun, just in case there was going to be any fun and games. The Russian who'd been guarding Pe outside drew his gun at the same time.

Velázquez moved in front of Pe and said, 'There's no need for anyone to get hurt here.'

Mr. Big didn't even turn to look back as he made his way over to the BMW, and his bodyguard went after him, walking backwards and keeping his gun pointed at Velázquez as he did so.

Velázquez kept his gun up as he watched the pair climb into the car. He watched them pull out and then drive off, without a shot being fired.

The next moment Pe was in his arms. 'Oh, Luis,' she sighed, 'I knew I could count on you.'

'I've been frantic, Pe... Did those bastards hurt you in any way?'

'No, they treated me okay.'

Velázquez said a silent prayer of thanks.

Now that he had Pe back safe and sound, Velázquez recalled that he'd meant to talk to Anna Segura again and drove over to the woman's flat. 'I'm afraid I'm busy,' she answered on the intercom when he identified himself.

'I promise not to take up much of your time... this is important.'

She buzzed him in, and Velázquez took the lift up to the third floor. He rang the bell and heard slippered feet scuffing over the tiles, then the oak door opened. As before, her slim form was clothed in tight black leggings and a top, and she'd caked her face in make-up. Her big dark eyes flashed him a look of sullen unwelcome from behind her long black tarantula lashes. 'I suppose you'd better come in,' she said, then took a step back to allow him to enter.

Velázquez was hit by the scent of jasmine as he passed through the door, and he went and stood before a black-and-white photograph of Calle Betis by night, taken from the other side of the Guadalquivir so that the lights of the bars and restaurants were reflected in the river. 'Take a seat, Inspector Jefe,' Anna Segura said. Velázquez parked himself on the Laura Ashley sofa.

Anna Segura reached down and took her Marlboros from the walnut coffee table, helped herself to one and then offered Velázquez the pack. 'No thanks,' he shook his head. 'I packed up five years ago.'

She shrugged. 'We've all got to die sooner or later.'

'Hopefully later.' Velázquez smiled.

She gave him a straight look then lit the cigarette, before she put the lighter back down on the coffee table. She found a small glass ashtray, and went and sat in one of the easy chairs. 'So what is it now, Inspector Jefe?'

'Your manuscript makes for fascinating reading,' he began. 'I wonder if I could talk to you about it some more?'

'Fire away.' She shrugged, then took a long drag on her Marlboro and deposited a few imaginary flakes of ash into the tray which was balanced on her lap.

'The part that tells Father Pedro's account of his past was of particular interest to me... Father Pedro wrote that section himself, I believe, didn't he?'

'What I'd like to know is why you're making such a big deal about this, Inspector Jefe?'

'I'm working on a murder case, señora Segura... four men have been murdered, two of them priests, and one of them was Father Pedro Mora, as I believe you already know.'

'But I really don't see what any of that has to do with me and my little book.' She took another long drag, and looked at Velázquez through a cloud of smoke, so that she reminded him briefly of some screen goddess from the past–Gloria Swanson, perhaps, in *Sunset Boulevard*. 'I mean, nothing that appears between the pages of my novel's gonna bring him back, right?'

'So it's a novel, then?'

'Yes.'

'Meaning that it's not fact, or what?'

'Did I say it was…?'

'Well, novels are fiction, right?'

'Correct.'

'Look, Señora Segura, I need you to come clean about this and tell me clearly and honestly, whether Father Pedro's account, as it appears in your manuscript, was written by him or by you, and whether it's all made up.'

Anna Segura's eyes flashed like warning signals through a thick fog. She thrashed her cigarette to death in the ashtray on her lap, looking at Velázquez as she did so. 'Okay,' she said, 'if it's so damned important then you may as well know—I lied to you… it's all fiction, every last bit of it… There. Are you happy now?'

'Including all of Father Pedro's account?'

'I said *all of it*, didn't I? Which one of those three short words was too long for you, Inspector Jefe?'

'So do you mean to say Father Pedro never killed General Balmes?'

'I said *fiction*, Inspector Jefe. There, I made it easier for you— that's only one word.'

'But why didn't you tell us that earlier?'

'I've no pension to speak of, and I've got to put some bread on the table the same as the next person.'

'You mean you only think your book will stand a chance of selling if people believe it's true history?'

Anna Segura seemed to shrug off her bitter attitude, the way a weary traveller drops her rucksack. 'Look,' she said, 'I'm sorry if I've wasted your time… The truth is, I feel rather ashamed of myself all of a sudden… I don't suppose it's much of an excuse, but I've got money worries and I thought the book might be a way of getting myself out of a hole if only I could get it published.'

If the woman wants to hear me tell her not to worry about

it, she's gonna have a long wait, Velázquez thought, as he got up and made for the door.

'Before you go, Inspector Jefe, there is one more thing that might be of interest to you.'

'I'm listening.'

'I was never involved with Father Pedro Mora, but I did know him. He's from Burgat originally, the village I'm from, and… well, there were rumours about him…'

'What sort of rumours?'

'Like I said, it was just a rumour—'

'Tell me about it.'

'There was talk that he'd abused a boy.'

'In Burgat?'

She nodded. 'I don't know if you know the village?'

'I've never been there, but I've heard of it. It's not too far from Ronda.'

'That's right, about half way between Ronda and the Costa del Sol. It's a tiny place, but most of the people who lived there back then have moved out by now. They had to in most cases, to find work.'

'What about Father Aloysius—was there a rumour about him, too?'

'No, he didn't live in Burgat.'

'When would this have been?'

'Back in the seventies, a year or two after General Franco died. I remember because I left the village in seventy-eight.'

'What was the name of the lad who was abused?'

'I never did find that out… like I say, it was just a rumour, and it was a long time ago.'

'If you can try to think back and remember any more about it, then I'd very much like to hear about it.' Velázquez reached into his jacket and brought out his card. 'You can reach me on this number.'

Anna Segura took the card and looked at it, and Velázquez went out.

CHAPTER 24

Burgat turned out to be little more than a bunch of whitewashed houses in a small valley, with a church positioned somewhere around the dip in the middle. The village was situated in the midst of a range of hills and mountains, roughly half way between Ronda and the coast. The countryside was surprisingly green in places.

Velázquez pulled into a dusty little parking area at the edge of the village, and he and Gajardo climbed out. The sun was doing its worst, and Velázquez could feel the sweat running down his back. 'I'll take the first house,' he said, 'and you take next door, Jose.'

They had worked their way down to the bottom of the hill before either of them came across anyone who'd been in the village for more than twenty-five years. Many of the properties appeared to be shut up, and they learned from residents that several were holiday homes.

Then they knocked on the door of a woman who told them her father had lived in the village all of his life. Velázquez asked if he might have a word with him, and was shown into the small living room where a man in his seventies was sitting in front of a television set. An old black and white Spanish film was showing. The woman told her father he had a visitor and invited Velázquez to take a seat. First Velázquez took out his ID and held it up for the man to see.

The man leaned forward to study it. Velázquez told the man that he was Jefe del Grupo de Homicidios in Seville, and that he was investigating the murders that had recently shocked the Andalusian capital.

The woman looked puzzled. 'So what are you doing in Burgat?'

191

'One of the victims was an old man who I have reason to believe lived in this village a long time ago—a Father Pedro Mora.'

'Yes, that's right,' the woman's father said. 'I remember him… I read about what happened to him in the newspaper.'

'What was he like when you knew him?'

The old man shrugged. 'Never knew him very well, to be honest.'

'But I should've thought everyone would have known each other in a small village like this in those days?'

'Yes, but I always kept my distance where he was concerned.'

'You mean you didn't like him or you aren't religious?'

'No, I'm not a believer, it's true… only it wasn't just that exactly.'

'What, then…?'

'He always seemed to have the bad milk… And besides, there were rumours about him.'

'Rumours…?'

'Yes… it was said he had tried to abuse a young boy in the village.'

'Did the police get involved?'

The old man shook his head. 'Far as I recall there were no witnesses, nothing was proven, you know… although nothing very bad actually happened as it turned out, because the boy escaped in time … Anyway, I kept my distance after I heard that.'

'When would this have been?'

'Oh, back in the seventies sometime. Not all that long after General Franco died.'

'Exactly how long after Franco's death?'

'A year or two, maybe.'

'What happened to the boy?'

'His family moved away… of course he would be a grown man now. Javier Moreno his name was. Went for a sailor he did, Javi, I later learned. His mother used to write to us every year, you see… but then the letters dried up and we learned that she'd passed away. Cancer.'

'Any idea how I might find this Javier Moreno?'

'On a navy vessel, I should imagine.'

Once he was in the street, the Inspector Jefe called Sara Pérez. '*Hola*, Sara, Velázquez here.'

'*Hola*, Boss.'

'You turned anything up yet?'

'Afraid not.'

'In that case, can you get onto the Admiralty and find out where a Javier Moreno is right now. Originally from Burgat.'

'Okay, I'll get on it now.'

'Thanks, Sara. And it's important, so call me back as soon as you have something.'

'Of course.'

They hung up and Velázquez went back to knocking on doors.

Just over an hour later, Officer Pérez called back. 'Tracked him down for you, Boss,' she said. 'He's on a ship that pulled into port down in Rota yesterday.'

'Got the name of the ship?'

'It's *El Principe*.'

'In that case get yourself down to Rota and talk to him on the double.'

'Already on my way, Boss.'

'Good work, Sara; be sure to call me as soon as you've talked to the man, okay?'

'Will do.'

They hung up.

Sub-inspector Gajardo emerged from the door of the next house at that moment, just in time to see Velázquez aim a punch at the sky. 'Got a result, Boss?'

'Very possibly, José,' Velázquez said. 'Pérez's on her way to talk to a man who might have been abused by Father Pedro Mora as a boy, back in the late seventies.'

'That does sound like a result.'

Heroin was buzzing in Velázquez's veins as they headed back to Seville. He'd shot up in the toilet of the only bar in Burgat before they left. His mobile began to ring, and he fished it out of his pocket. '*Hola?*'

'Luis, it's Luz. Good news—they've managed to decode the encryption.'

'You mean you've been able to watch the CD-Rom?'

'Sure have, and it's what you thought it would be like,' Luz said. 'Just like the other one, only in this one you can see the faces...'

'Recognize any of the men on it?'

'Those two young gay guys who were shot in bed... I remember their faces from the photographs they put in the newspapers.'

'Who else?'

'That politician guy... what's-his-name–Villalba.'

'He's dead too. Who else?'

'And then there's the Mayor's lawyer, Alfonso Cayetano-Fitzmorgan; I know him because my friend was dating his son for a while.'

'He's still alive,' Velázquez said, thinking aloud. 'At least, he is so far as I know...'

'You think he could be next on the killer's hit list, right?'

'I'd bet my salary on it.'

'In that case, I suppose you'll be wanting to know where he lives,' Luz said.

'Do you mean to say you have an address?'

'I thought you might need it, so I did a little research to save you time.'

'You're a gem, Luz. Did anyone ever tell you that?'

Luz chuckled and said, 'Man's got a big place over on Calle Bailen.'

'Know the number?'

Luz told him.

'We're on our way over there to talk to him now. Thanks for the good work, Luz.'

Velázquez hung up and dropped his mobile onto his lap, then he put his foot down. And they had just reached the outskirts of Seville, minutes later, when his phone began to ring again. *'Hola?'*

'Pérez, Boss.'

'You found Javier Moreno yet?'

'Just been talking to the man.'

'And...?'

'Said Father Pedro Mora tried to rape him when he was eleven, but he managed to get away from him. Javier Moreno says he told his family what happened, and his father went to the police. Apparently officers in Ronda spoke to Father Pedro, but he denied it all and that was as far as the investigation went.'

'How long was Moreno away at sea?'

'Just got back from a three-month return trip to Argentina only yesterday... which means he obviously couldn't've killed Fathers Pedro or Aloysius.'

'No, but he could've got somebody else to do it for him.'

'Suppose it's possible... although I must say he didn't seem the type.'

'Killers rarely do.'

'Oh yes, I almost forgot,' she said. 'One curious thing that I turned up—Javier Moreno happens to be the brother of Father Antonio, the priest who serves at the Iglesia de Jesus del Gran Poder... apparently the priest had his surname changed to Dominguez some years ago.'

'My God, it's all fitting into place now.'

'What is, Boss?'

'No time to explain, Sara. I'll fill you in on the details later.'

Velázquez hung up and put his foot down.

Alfonso Cayetano-Fitzmorgan's place was an old five-storey palace of the sort that had once been home to the city's aristocratic elite.

There was no response at the buzzer, so Velázquez picked the lock to get the front door open. That set the burglar alarm off, but Gajardo soon found it. They heard the distant murmur of voices; followed it to the study, where they found Alfonso Cayetano-Fitzmorgan and Father Antonio Dominguez. The priest was holding a gun, and he had it pointed at the lawyer. '*Hola*, Inspector Jefe,' he said. 'I wondered when you were going to catch up with me.'

'Put the gun down, Father Antonio.'

'I can't do that, I'm afraid… you see, this man is an abuser of children.'

'I know all about that.'

'How did you find out?'

'I know about the CD-Rom,' Velázquez said. 'Not the one you gave me, but the one where you get to see the men's faces… And everyone who was on the film has already been murdered, with the exception of this man and the boy who was being raped.'

'This man is sick. He needs to die.'

'Come on, Father, priests aren't meant to kill people… you know that.'

'You think I'm crazy, is that it?'

Velázquez didn't say anything.

'Of course you do,' continued Father Antonio. 'Many people would have it that religious faith itself is nothing more than a form of structured mass insanity anyway… What is prayer, after all, they argue, but talking to someone who isn't there? Well, I'm here to tell you that the atheists are wrong, Inspector Jefe.

God *does* exist… and he needs people to carry out his work here on Earth, as you policemen seem incapable of doing it.'

'Father Antonio,' Velázquez said, 'why don't you put the gun down and we can talk about all this at our leisure…?'

'You'd like that, wouldn't you? You'd like me to let this servant of Satan off, so that he'll be free to do more evil, is that it?'

'I'd like him to have a fair trial, and then to be sent to prison for a very long time for his crimes.'

'His lawyer would probably get him off, Inspector Jefe… and even if he did get put away, he'd probably be out within a few years if he kept his nose clean.'

'Listen, Father Antonio, I know the system isn't perfect but it's the best hope we have of creating a decent and civilized society… Murder is wrong, Father. That's another thing I know. And if you think God wants you to kill this man, if He is up there looking down on this little scene, then I think you're wrong… And anyway, what about the idea of redemption…? Doesn't it say in the Bible that every man should be given the opportunity to redeem himself?'

'Yes, but it also stresses the need to stamp out Satan.'

'Strikes me that you're trying to play God, Father Antonio… Now why don't you tell me about the other men on the CD-Rom? Did you kill them, too?'

'God wanted it so… They were servants of Satan.'

'What about Fathers Pedro and Aloysius?'

'They were the same… They weren't on the CD-Rom, but I already knew about all them and their sick perversions.'

'One thing that confuses me, Father—why did you change your *modus operandi* after killing the two priests?'

'I wanted to give you the impression that there was more than one killer out there, Inspector Jefe.'

'And from what I've seen, I wonder if you hated the priests just that little bit more than your other victims? Is that why you killed them the way you did?' Velázquez exchanged glances with Gajardo, and then, before Father Antonio could reply, the two officers lunged at him. Alfonso Cayetano-Fitzmorgan dived onto the floor and the priest fired the gun. The bullet got Alfonso Cayetano-Fitzmorgan in the leg, and he cried out.

The next moment, Velázquez was wrestling Father Antonio for the gun. Gajardo came at the priest from behind, then the two detectives wrestled him to the floor, and the Inspector Jefe was able to disarm him.

Velázquez took out his mobile and called for an ambulance, while Gajardo put a pair of plastic restraints on Father Antonio's wrists.

CHAPTER 25

That evening, Velázquez and Pe Naranjo were sitting on high stools with José Gajardo at the long wooden counter in the Bar Eslava, drinking red wine and eating tapas. The place was packed to the seams, and people were jammed in at their back, so that the waiters had to keep handing dishes over and between them. The waiters were kept busy with a constant stream of orders, and they worked fast but with a cheerful sort of grace under pressure, calling out orders, collecting dishes, handing them over the counter; somehow managing to know what it was each customer owed when the time came for the bill. The owner was a cheerful sort of presence behind the bar, too, and many of the smart people in the town had come here to enjoy the excellent food. Velázquez was feeling good about things in general, now that he had Pe back safe and sound. Pe was a marvellous woman, and maybe he wasn't such a bad guy himself, and Seville was a damn fine city, and the Bar Eslava was a hell of a good bar to be in, especially if you were eating *calamares* and *jamon serrano*, and *solomillo de buey* and *chuletas de cordero* and stuffed *aceitunas*, and a few other things they'd eaten between them that he couldn't remember right now, all washed down with a pretty damned decent red. He was feeling happy. He'd had a difficult moment or two a little earlier, but he'd taken a shot of methadone and now he was feeling as strong as a bull.

'So, what set Father Antonio on his killing spree?' Pe asked.

Velázquez picked up the wine bottle and replenished their glasses. 'You tell it, José,' he said.

Gajardo sipped his wine. 'The man was raped repeatedly by a priest at the orphanage as a boy.'

'Bit odd that he should've decided to enter the priesthood

himself in that case, isn't it?'

'Way he saw it his abuser, Father Miguel, served Satan, and Father Antonio wanted to serve God—'

'And for him,' Velázquez cut in, 'that meant killing all the bad priests.'

'The paedophile priests he knew of, you mean?'

'Exactly.'

Pe looked puzzled. 'Still don't get what led you to him, though.'

'All really started to fall into place when we discovered Father Pedro Mora had tried to rape a boy by the name of Javier Moreno, back in the seventies,' Velázquez replied. 'And then we found out that this Javier Moreno's actually Father Antonio's brother, only he changed his surname to Dominguez a few years back.'

'Then we found him at Alfonso Cayetano-Fitzmorgan's house when he got there,' Gajardo added.

'But what made you think of going there in the first place?'

'We wanted to talk to him.'

'Who, Alfonso Cayetano or Father Antonio?'

'Both…that is, we went there to talk to Cayetano, but the priest just happened to be there already.'

'And he was about to kill Cayetano…?'

'Got there just in time,' Velázquez put in.

'But I still don't get what Cayetano had to do with it all… Is he a paedophile, too?'

'That's right.'

'But what was it that put you onto him?'

Velázquez popped a piece of cod into his mouth, swallowed. 'He was one of the men on the CD-Rom.'

'CD-Rom…?'

'Containing footage of a young boy being repeatedly raped.'

'I see.' Pe's brow furrowed as she took it all in. 'Why did the Russians who kidnapped me want a CD-Rom with some paedophiles on it so badly?'

'To use to blackmail Cayetano,' Velázquez replied. 'Man's a big cheese at the Town Hall.'

'Or was.' Gajardo grinned. 'Where he's headed he's going to end up being someone's breakfast if he isn't careful.'

'Meaning you've got enough proof to put him away?'

'He's made a full confession.'

'Case solved, then.' Pe sipped her wine. 'Sounds like you two have had a rather successful day.'

'You can say that again.' Velázquez popped an olive into his mouth.

'Better not do that,' Pe smiled. 'It might go to your head.'

Gajardo glanced at his watch. 'Is that the time,' he said. 'I'd better be off.'

'Got a hot date?'

'Something like that.'

'Enjoy the rest of your evening, José.'

'Thanks… you two, as well.' He reached for his wallet. 'How much do I owe for the food and wine?'

'It's on us,' Velázquez said.

When Gajardo had left, Velázquez turned to Pe and smiled. 'I feel so bad about what happened to you,' he said.

'No need to feel like that, Luis. Wasn't your fault.'

'I'm not so sure about that… I mean, the Russian only kidnapped you to get at me.'

'That's true, I suppose… but I always knew you'd come and get me.' She chewed on a juicy chunk of cod before swallowing it. 'I know the kind of man you are.'

'What kind of man's that?'

She grinned. 'The sort that always takes the bull by the horns when the chips are down.'

Velázquez felt Pe's hand easing up his thigh, and he thought how gorgeous she looked. 'Do you make a habit of that, Pe?'

'What… feeling men up, you mean?'

Velázquez's mobile began to vibrate in his pocket. He took it out and said, 'No, mixing your metaphors…'

'*Diga?*'

'Great work, Inspector Jefe.'

It was Diego Blanco.

'News travels fast, I see.'

'Dog can't take a poop in the street in this city without I get to know about it.'

'So it seems.'

'Must be feeling pretty happy with yourself.'

'Guess so,' Velázquez said. 'Although I still haven't managed to find out who Bill and the Black Lady were.'

'Bill and *who*...?'

'Couple of nutters who stole my car a while back.' Among other things, Velázquez thought.

'Prob'ly working for the Russians and wanted you off their case.'

'Your answer to most things, Diego, right?'

'Only because it's true... Anyway, just thought I'd call to congratulate you on an excellent piece of police work, Inspector Jefe... And I see that Alfonso Cayetano-Fitzmorgan's been charged, so the Russians won't be able to use the CD-Rom to blackmail him now his secret's out.'

'That's true.'

'Don't be fooled, though—this is one battle you've won, but the war with the Russians is still far from over... Any time you need my help to run them out of town, you only have to call...'

'I'll bear it in mind.'

'Be sure to stay in touch.'

'Don't worry, I will.'

Pe said, 'Who was that?'

'Oh, just someone calling to congratulate me on solving the case.'

Pe sipped her Rioja and smiled. 'It's so great to be free and back together again, Luis.'

Velázquez took her hand in his and gave it a tender squeeze.

'You're too right it is,' he said in a voice that was raspy with emotion. 'I don't know what I would've done without you, Pe.' He'd said stuff like that to girls before, but this was the first time he'd ever meant it. And there was something strange going on in his chest: a funny hollow sensation he'd never experienced before. I'm really in love this time, he thought. And all of a sudden he had the urge to ask Pe to marry him. Why not? he thought. If you can't marry Pe then you should never marry anyone. Because you'll never find another girl that you'll love like this one.

He wondered, though, if he was the marrying type. Remembered the joke that said a cop should never allow himself to get handcuffed, and wondered if there were some truth in it…

Of course you're not the marrying type, he told himself. But neither's Pe. So that kinda levels things up. Besides, we've always found a way of figuring things out between us in the past. One way and another. I love her and she loves me. That's the important thing.

'Pe,' he began, nervous as a love-struck schoolboy. Then his mobile began to vibrate in his breast pocket.

He decided to ignore it.

'Pe,' he said, 'there's something I've been meaning to talk to you about…'

'Your mobile's ringing.'

'I know.'

'Well…aren't you going to answer it?'

'Yes, but—'

'It might be something important, Luis.'

He reached into his breast pocket and took it out. '*Hola?*'

A female voice he didn't recognize said, 'Is that Inspector Jefe Velázquez…?'

'Speaking.'

'We haven't met, Inspector, but I'm Carmen Segura… I

hope you don't mind me calling you on your mobile like this, but I wanted to talk to you on behalf of my mother, Anna. You interviewed her recently, she told me, concerning a murder case.'

'Yes, on two occasions to be exact.'

'She told me about it.'

'So what can I do for you, *señorita*?'

'My mother has passed away and… well, I thought you ought to know.'

'Oh, I'm terribly sorry… But when did it happen?'

'Only a couple of hours ago,' Carmen Segura said.

'There's no hint of foul play, I hope?'

'Oh no, nothing like that, Inspector Jefe… I think she'd got herself very stressed ever since she started writing the book she was working on… She'd had a stroke… and then she had what I later learned was a massive heart attack just before the ambulance arrived.'

'I'm very sorry, *señorita*… please allow me to pass on my condolences.'

'Thank you, Inspector… but I'm really calling because my mother seemed to be very troubled about something she'd said to you.'

'Oh… what was that?'

'She clearly wanted to talk, but she was rambling, so I didn't understand much… I did understand, though, that she wanted me to call and tell you that she'd written a letter to you.'

'I see… what's in the letter?'

'I'm not totally sure… the letter's sealed, and I wouldn't open it for the world. But my mother did tell me that she'd lied to you, Inspector, and this seemed to be troubling her.'

'Did she give you any specific details?'

'No, she was rambling, like I said… All I know is it had something to do with Father Pedro Mora and a General Balmes.'

'I see… so perhaps you can send me the letter, then?'

'I can do better than that—if you'd like to come to the funeral tomorrow morning, I'll hand it to you in person.'

'Yes, that would be most kind.'

'The funeral will take place at eleven a.m., at the cemetery in Seville.'

'Okay, I'll see you there, *señorita* Segura. Thank you very much for the call… and please allow me to pass on my condolences once more to you and your family.'

'Thank you, Inspector. Until tomorrow, then.'

They hung up.

Pe shot him a puzzled look, and Velázquez brought her up to speed. Then he paid the bill.

It was just a short walk back to the flat on Calle Teodosio, and as soon as they got in Velázquez took Pe in his arms. 'You don't know how much I've…' He was lost for words.

'What's the matter, Inspector Jefe?' Pe said. 'Something about your behaviour gives me the impression you want to make a powder.'

'I want to make love to you,' he said.

'Same thing, no?'

He grinned. 'How about we do it and find out?'

They tore each other's clothes off.

EPILOGUE

There were only four other people at the funeral the following morning, apart from Velázquez and the priest: an old lady who looked like she must be Anna Segura's sister, two other younger women, and a man of around the same age as the women. Inspector Jefe didn't recognize any of them.

Velázquez eyed the two younger women furtively as the priest said the last rites, and wondered which of them was Carmen Segura—the one in the trouser suit, or the one in the long black dress?

As soon as the service was concluded, the woman in the black trouser suit came over and introduced herself. 'I'm the woman that called you yesterday, Inspector Jefe,' she said. 'Thank you for coming.'

'The least I could do,' Velázquez replied.

'I've brought this for you, like I promised.' She reached inside her jacket, brought out a letter and handed it to Velázquez. 'As I told you yesterday, Inspector,' Carmen Segura said, 'Mother seemed to be most troubled by the fact that she'd lied to you about something to do with Father Pedro Mora and this General Balmes, so I suspect it's about that.'

Velázquez opened the letter. It had been typed on two sheets of A4 paper.

He began to read:

Dear Inspector Jefe Velázquez,

I find that my conscience is troubled on account of some of the things I told you, and so I find I really must finally set the record straight.

To begin with, it's true that I was courted by a young man on Tenerife in the summer of 1936, and the young man in question did, to the very best of my knowledge, assassinate General Balmes; only the man involved was not Pedro Mora—or Father Pedro— but somebody quite different.

I was very much in love with the young man in question at the time, although I don't think I realized just how deeply until much later, by which time everything had gone wrong: the egg had been smashed, as it were, and by then there was no putting the pieces that made up the shell back together again, as there never is.

So I must apologize, Inspector Jefe, for having lied to you on two accounts: firstly when I told you that the man in my manuscript was the young Father Pedro Mora; and then a second time, when I told you that I'd made everything in my manuscript up and that it was all fiction.

The parts that I told you had been written by Pedro Mora were in fact written by my first love. He had his son trace me somehow, and sent his account to me through the post. He was dying of cancer and very near the end at the time, and I rushed to the hospital and was at least able to spend a little time with him before he passed away.

He assured me that everything he wrote in the account he sent me was true. Almendralejo, joining the Republicans and the maquis in the Pyrenees… And he further assured me that what I'd heard my father telling my mother that day, in the summer of 1936, was also true: he had indeed killed General Balmes, thereby kick-starting the Civil War.

I see no reason to create a lot of stress and bother for his children by telling you his name; it is sufficient, I think, for me simply to tell you what really happened, and this I have now done.

Well, there it is. I subsequently married another man who bore me two lovely daughters, before he died five years ago.

That's all there is to tell. I feel better now that I've finally told you the truth, and got the whole thing off my chest (even though you won't actually get to read this letter until after I have passed away). I hate lying and liars, you see, and have always done my best to be honest all my life.

You strike me as being a good man, Inspector Jefe, and that only made the thought of having lied to you play on my conscience all the more.

I wish you well from beyond the grave.

With best regards,

Anna Segura

AUTHOR'S NOTE:

I have used a small number of Spanish English phrases very sparingly throughout the book; while the original meaning may be obvious from the context, the following list gives a more in-depth meaning to each phrase used for those readers keen to understand more of Spanish idioms and culture.

GLOSSARY OF IDIOMATIC SPANISH ENGLISH TERMS & VOCABULARY

He gave her a pair of horns (p. 13)—he cheated on her (i.e. when speaking of adultery)

Horse—heroin (ps. 80, 82)

Just throwing/to throw water into the sea (p. 14)—It (whatever is being talked about) is pointless or a waste of time.

Son of the great whore (ps. 104,133, 149, 240): where we would say 'son of a bitch'.

Up to his nuts (p.213)—at the end of his tether/had it up to here. (This is a slight tweaking of the Spanish phrase *Hasta la coronilla* (Literally: *Until the crown of my head*) or the more colloquial *hasta los cojones* (*Literally: until the balls*).

Taking me by the hair (ps 98, 113)—Taking the mickey, poking fun

Shouting like a *toro* (p 15) serves as an intensifier, hence: to shout as loudly as a bull.

She/He was turned into a chili (p 149)—He/she was very angry or hopping mad.

The woman of my heart (p 156)—the woman I love.

When you build a house it's best not to start with the roof (p113)—Roughly the equivalent of 'Don't put the cart before the horse'.

He dirtied/shat in the milk of the man's ancestors (p.208)—The most offensive insult in Spanish: literally the speaker is expressing his wish to defecate in the milk of his interlocutor's ancestors. (The Spanish seem to have an obsession with breast milk—in linguistic terms, anyway—and they use the word 'leche' (milk) in a number of different ways.)

…shitting in the milk (ps 76, 84); He shat in the milk (ps. 96, 192)—This is another way of saying 'He cursed' (i.e. here Velázquez is cursing under his breath, and no specific insult is aimed at any one individual).

To have drunk/drink the bad milk (ps 119, 129, 240, 250)—To be in a bad mood.

To make a powder (p. 265) to fuck, to make love

You threw the house through the window (p37) — you went all out/pulled out all the stops

Vocabulary

aceitunas—olives

adios—goodbye

Agente—the police rank below Subinspector but above Oficial

café con leche—coffee with milk

calamares—squid (usually served as rings of squid fried in batter)

carajillo—coffee with brandy

chuletas de cordero—lamb chops

Científicos (abbreviation of Policía Científica)—These use modern scientific techniques to analyze the crime scene, or objects taken from it, in the search for DNA, fingerprints etc.

cojones—used alone this is an expletive, meaning 'balls'. If a person 'has cojones', though, they are very brave.

Comisario—the Chief Inspector's boss

diga—say/speak: people often use this single word when answering the telephone.

gracias—thank you

guapa—pretty

hasta luego—See you later

hola—hello

hombre—man

iglesia—Church

Inspector Jefe—Chief Inspector

Inspector Jefe del Grupo de Homicidios—Chief Inspector in charge of the Homicide Department

jamon serrano—cured Spanish ham

Jefatura—police headquarters

joder—fuck

Médico Forense—pathologist: the doctor who performs autopsies.

mierda—shit

Oficial—the lowest police rank

plaza—square (often lined with pavement cafes in Spain).

poli—cop

querida—my love/beloved

solomillo de buey—sirloin taken from the ox

Subinspector—the rank below Chief Inspector, roughly equivalent perhaps to Detective Sergeant

te quiero—I love you

toro—bull

Printed in May 2023
by Rotomail Italia S.p.A., Vignate (MI) - Italy